The Great Master
of Ecstasy

Glenda Beagan

seren

Seren is the book imprint of
Poetry Wales Press Ltd
57 Nolton Street, Bridgend, Wales, CF31 3AE
www.seren-books.com

ISBN: 9-781-85411-487-7

Inner design and typesetting by books@lloydrobson.com

Printed by Bell and Bain, Glasgow

The publisher works with the financial assistance of
the Welsh Books Council.

Contents

The Great Master of Ecstasy

one

Not that kind of ecstasy?

No?

No. Definitely not. It's not necessary.

I sit at the little table under the skylight. It's brilliant up here in the clouds. Well, that's a bit of an exaggeration I suppose. Clouds. More like chimney pots and aerials. Kieran tells me to use words properly, weighing each one like a precious stone.

Have you never taken anything, then?

Years ago I tried this and that: had a couple of bad trips. Some people need stuff to get out of their heads.

And you don't?

I can be wherever I want to be.

You make it sound easy.

Kieran just smiles. I shut up. I must be bothering him with all this chat and I'm frightened he'll send me away. Though I don't think he will. He never has. He's so patient. Now, as I sit here watching him sketching, it's as if I can hear his mind hushing me. I'm glad to know my chat doesn't bother him. And I know why it doesn't. He's centred. He hasn't got a monkey mind like the rest of us. His is a deep quiet well. So although he makes it sound so easy, I know it isn't. I know how many years he's studied. How many masters he's sat at

the feet of, though when I said that to him he just laughed
and said he'd never sit at the feet of anyone. Anyway he's a
proper shaman now. People consult him.

He hires a room at the Yoga Centre, Wednesdays and Saturday mornings.

I found this definition of a shaman in a book about Native
American tribal lore. Quoting Mircea Eliade (I thought that
was the name of a woman!), it said that the term shaman
refers to 'the great master of ecstasy'.

I loved that. Even the sound of it gave me a buzz. I said
it to myself over and over. The book went on to say that
the shaman 'specialises in a trance during which his soul is
believed to leave his body and ascend to the sky or descend to
the underworld'.

And I know that when Kieran says he can be wherever he
wants to be, he means exactly what he says.

His flat is weird but it's got a good feeling to it. It's on the
fourth floor. In the attics. The ceilings slope and all the
windows are skylights. There are no blinds, so at night, with
the house being so tall, high above most of that orangey town
glow, you can lie in your bed and swim in the moonlight.
That's what it feels like. Now I've got my own place I'm never
here at night which is a shame because I miss that feeling of
being way up in the sky among the stars. At the time of the full
moon her face seems to peer right down at you, just above
your head. I always think of the moon as a she.

The first time I came to Kieran's flat was when Kieran
rescued me. That sounds a bit dramatic but it's true. I'd been
sleeping rough all summer which wasn't bad, in fact I liked
it. I found good places, one was on what's left of the dunes
behind the lifeboat station, and the other was in the Jubilee

Gardens. When they were closing I'd make sure I was well out of it, hiding by the incinerator thing next to all those greenhouses at the back.

But winter came all at once and it was a different story then. I don't want to talk about the way I was when Kieran found me, or what I'd been doing just to keep going; I owe him a lot.

I was really ill. I had this really bad bronchitis. And I'd got this skin infection; my skin was kind of peeling and wet. Kieran isn't into doctors, not ordinary doctors, but he knows herbalists and people like that. He got me eating properly for the first time in years. Then nearly three months later he got me to write to my parents, just to say I was still alive. He was going to Manchester to take part in a 'sweat lodge' and he posted the letter there. I made him promise. I didn't want them to know where I was, so I had to be sure my letter was going to be posted far enough away. Even then I didn't completely trust him. I can't believe that after all he'd done for me I still had doubts. I grabbed his hands and looked up into his eyes to read them.

All I saw was honesty.

From the skylight in the little living room/kitchen you can see across the rooftops to the hills. They look blue and gentle. Sometimes misted, like a Chinese painting, sometimes sharp and clear. You get this illusion that they're so close you could reach out to touch them.

And then there's the top of the catholic church like a great shark's fin.

Wow, I said, Jaws. Just look at that!

This was the first time I'd felt strong enough to stand and peer out of the window without being propped up.

Stupidly, like a big kid, I started to mimic the music from the film – DUH DUH, DUH DUH, DUH DUH, DUH DUH.

It's good to see you can be silly, Kieran said.

When I was able to get out a bit I found the church, Our Lady of the Assumption. It's opposite the Yoga Centre. Sometimes on Wednesdays when Kieran was at the centre I'd get really bored and restless in the flat. I'd go to wait for him outside in that little Zen garden, all raked gravel and stones. I'd rake that gravel myself, for something to do, and I got to like it, the way all the rippling lines formed in those little whitish stones. The rake was wood, all wood, even the teeth of it, and these were widely spaced to make the right patterns.

If it rained I'd go and sit in the church. It's a modern build-ing, a peculiar shape from the outside, like a wonky pyramid, and it was the topmost tip of this you could see looking like a shark's fin from Kieran's window. I'd turn round there on the pavement and look up over the roofs to see if I could make out which was his flat. I couldn't be sure though. There were so many houses that looked all the same, tall and kind of grand originally, I should think, when they were all boarding houses and people hadn't heard of the Costa Brava. Or Florida. Now all these houses are multiple lets. There's lots of druggies.

Kieran says he doesn't pay much rent for his place partly because of the street it's in which has got a bad reputation (even us dossers had heard it was a place to keep clear of) and partly because it's right at the top of the building, with those funny wedge-shaped rooms. But it's exactly those things that make the place special and Kieran has got it so nice, all painted white with lots of trailing ivies and ferns in glass bells. And on the skylights he's hung pendants on leather straps. They work like mobiles, all different shapes and colours, with silver edges and silver spirals on them.

The spiral is a sacred shape. Kieran's shown me pictures of this great gravestone at Newgrange in Ireland, and it's covered with spirals. The place is so old it's even older than Stonehenge. I'd love to go there.

Kieran does a lot of sketching. He calls them his preliminaries. He gets the ideas of people's totem animals from their consultations with him. I know he doesn't charge people much for these sessions, only what he thinks they can afford, but he does make quite a bit of money from his artwork sometimes. He gets commissions and he says it's surprising how many people have owl totems. The way he paints them they're all different. They're magic. They don't look as if they're painted at all and they don't look as if they're on a flat surface either. You feel you could touch those feathers and they'd be real feathers. You feel those owls could rise up out of their frames and fly.

Once he painted a special commission for an American living in London. He was a financier or something. I asked Kieran how on earth he'd got to know this bloke who was rolling in money. Apparently he'd seen Kieran's advertisement somewhere. I didn't know he advertised.

You won't find my ads in magazines in the corner shop, he said. They're in specialist journals.

I teased him then for sounding so stuck-up and posh! But it also made me realise there was another aspect to Kieran, one I didn't know anything about. Anyway, this painting was completed and sent off but came right back because it was undelivered: Return to Sender kind of thing. I'd have been very angry, all that wasted time and energy. Kieran wasn't. He said there must be a reason. I got the feeling he somehow knew that the man was dead.

You could sell it to someone else, I said. It's beautiful.

Kieran shook his head. He set the painting up on the mantlepiece. It was a pair of elf owls on a cactus. These are the tiniest owls you could imagine, very pretty with big golden eyes. In the painting the cactus has a hole in its side where one of the owls is peeping out. It's obvious its nest is there, right inside. The flesh of the cactus itself is a yellowy green, ridged and a bit blotchy but one section is ablaze with flowers. These are almost as big as the owls themselves, like sunflowers, with crowns of white petals and yellow middles.

Did he describe them to you or did you have a picture to work from? I asked him.

As soon as he told me what he wanted I imagined how they were, he said.

Kieran is often matter of fact and mysterious at the same time.

When I was ill I slept in Kieran's bed and somehow he managed to sleep on the thin lumpy sofa in the other room. The bedroom skylight looked out towards the sea and although you couldn't see it with all the buildings in between, you knew it was there because the light was different, brighter and whiter. I think it was being with Kieran that made me notice things like this. I'm sure I never used to. Now I saw things, really saw things. I saw the shine on the top rim of the Big Wheel on the horizon, and on a clear evening when the wind was blowing the right way I could hear the far squeals and howls of the Ghost Train. And I watched the gulls do their aerial acrobatics. Before, when I'd heard all their squawkings, it was just a noise to me. It got on my nerves. Now it seemed there was a kind of music in it, and this music had moods: sad, happy, pensive. I was sensitive to everything around me, everything I touched. Everything that touched me. When I told Kieran about this he said it was because I'd been so ill. Now it was like everything was new.

I admit that once I was better I expected him to sleep with me. I took it for granted he would. I mean I'm not ugly or anything. But he wasn't interested. I felt rejected. I wanted to say thank you for everything he'd done for me and what else had I got to give him? I began to think he was gay or something. I had so much to learn.

But once I was better, really better, he suggested I look for a place of my own. He came with me to fill in forms and everything so I could get some income support. I felt guilty. He'd fed me all this time and had never asked for a penny. I'd never really thought about what it was costing him.

The problem I had with you was getting you to eat in the first place, he said.

Even when I got my own bedsit and started on a back-to-work course (IT and Business Admin), I still went to see him. I was nervous at first. Yes, he'd got me well again, got me back on my feet, but perhaps he wouldn't want to see me anymore.

He did though. Who needs that other kind of ecstasy?

Things changed now. It wasn't like I was dependent, the way I'd been. We were more sort of equal, though how could anybody be equal with Kieran? Now we talked about what he believed in, what being a shaman was all about. He was teaching me, only it wasn't like being taught. With Kieran I just absorbed information. I learned about the Lakota Sioux medicine man he'd worked with. I learned about Taoism and the Aborigine Dreamtime. Then there was Cuchulain, the Hound of Ulster, and Finn: all those Irish heroes. I learned about The Matter of Britain, about runes and rituals and the great web of wyrd, about the guardian skulls Kieran had seen lodged in the chimney breasts of old farms.

All those things that Kieran talked to me about he treated all the same. What I mean is that he didn't make out that some things were more important than others. Or that some things were personal to him, part of his own experience. They were though.

I always believed that when you were dead you were dead. Finished. End of story. I don't now.

I remember it all as if it were a bad dream. Not real. Jon and Vanda from the Yoga Centre came round to tell me. It was early morning. They'd found him in the garden when they went to open up and he must have been lying there overnight, he'd lost so much blood. Some people must have gone for him after he'd finished his consultations. Thought he had a lot of money on him, druggies I suppose. We reckon there must have been at least two of them, and that they must have been waiting for him.

I couldn't understand how anyone could hurt Kieran. I sat by his bed in the hospital listening to the ventilator breathing for him, looking at all those tubes. Already I felt he wasn't there, that this was just his shell. I knew it was just a matter of time before they switched off that machine.

The landlord asked me to clear Kieran's flat. I sat there in the half dark, thinking about him, looking at his painting of the elf owls. Then, as I watched, they seemed to glow, even move a little. The pendants on the skylights tinkled. The spiral shapes shone on the walls around, shone and danced and circled, then all those ivies and ferns, their shadows. Everything seemed to be dancing. A warm bright wind suddenly seemed to be blowing through the room with, just for a second or two, a quick shift of light in the painting. I don't care if you don't believe me. I don't expect you to, but for just a moment I felt an owl alight on my shoulder. I felt its feathers, its little hard cold beak touching my face.

two

The road ahead of him kept plunging down and away from him, faster, steeper, way, way and down from him, down from under his feet, running now in the cool air, the sound his shoes made on the road like drumming, all the time faster and faster on the steepness of the hill, as if he would either take off and fly or fall flat on his face, and either way it didn't matter, his favourite place for running in the world, and no one would know why, just see, only there was no one about anyway, and he was hidden under the trees, just see a boy running, a kind of game but it wasn't, wouldn't know why or how it made him feel either, running faster and faster and down and down under the blackly green, the greenly black tunnel, the hood of the holly trees.

And sometimes, when it was bad, he would see what he'd seen when he came home from school that day, when he'd let himself in with his key and found her there, lying there, half in the hall, half still on the stairs, her arms and legs all over the place, and her head up against the sticking-out part of the banister at the foot of the stairs. And he knew straightaway she was dead.

And sometimes when it was good, where the road began to flatten out again and light came bursting in, a sharp shaft of it, a bit like a flickering of tiny fishes in the jaggedy mirrors of the holly leaves, (and all because the holly trees were not like a tunnel now but had gaps so the sky showed and it was thinner) there was a dappled light on the road. Like the light of a shadow, very quick and dancing. And he knew it was his mother. Bonnie. He'd always called her Bonnie, never mum. She didn't like being called mum.

Bonnie, he'd say, under his breath, though he knew shadows don't speak. Still, in the silvery-edged movements of the shadow there was something like words, a message for him. It was like the feeling of being in a safe place. Though he always wanted the feeling, it couldn't last, so it didn't really make him feel any better in the end. It was hatred that made him feel better, not this sad feeling. He hated it when the bullies in school made fun of him. The worst of them were Dermot Roberts and Wayne Craig. He could see their faces now and he hated them. Scouser, they shouted. Dirty Scouse scally. Thinking about Bonnie made him feel as if he was shrinking. Like he was turning into water and going down the drain. Thinking about Dermot and Wayne drew out of him a strong clear current of hate. And it strengthened him, this hate, glued all the bits of him together again so he felt solid again. And real.

A little further on and the hood of the holly trees was finished. All sky and openness now, above low hedges. And a yellowhammer clicketing in an oak tree. As he looked up at the bird (he did not know its name then, or even the name of the tree, but he loved the bird's bright, almost canary, colour) he saw what was surely a serpent. Straight out of the Garden of Eden, coiled along the whole length of the oak tree's lowest branch. He picked up a stone from the road, a plain ordinary stone and he threw it at the glittering serpent with all his strength. Nothing happened. The stone had no effect on it at all, though he'd definitely hit it. He chose another stone, a bigger one that felt good in his hand. And this time he caught the serpent on the head. A kind of energy just like a wave rushed down its whole length. It lost its purchase on the tree. It fell at his feet, no longer a supple body with life shining in it. It was simply an empty snakeskin. He bent down to pick it up but there was nothing there. Where it had lain on the road there was nothing at all.

He looked around him and he was scared. He sensed something was different, that someone was there.

Why do you maim my creature? a voice with an echo in it called out to him. A man stood ahead of him on the road. He had a dark shape that seemed to have no proper edges and although the shape was dark it somehow hurt your eyes to look at it. As if it was actually bright, like looking at the sun.

The boy's mind tried to answer though no sound at all came out of his mouth. He was trying to say that he didn't know why he'd done it and he definitely wouldn't do it again but he had no voice at all, not even a squeak. Who are you? was the question his mind made and the bright dark man answered him: I am the holly king.

three

The boy came to Celynnen in the small dark hours. He knew his mother was dead. He knew this man driving him through the night was her brother, Bryn. Bonnie'd said she had a brother, but she'd never said anything else about him. And now this man, this Uncle Bryn, told him he'd seen him once before, long ago. The boy couldn't remember. You were only a baby then, said Bryn.

It is dark and starlight.

So much you don't know when you're nine years old and your life is splintering. You don't know that out of all these splinters something so different will grow that you will hardly recognise this self you have become. You have been made by one place. Now you will be made by another.

It was a long way to drive to wherever they were going. It was the middle of the night of the most terrible day of his life. He was very tired but he didn't want to fall asleep. It was as if he didn't dare close his eyes on the world ever again. But he must have fallen asleep in the end and now he woke suddenly, not knowing where he was or what was happening. Then he remembered. Oh no, he remembered. Most of all though he wanted to wee. The car was hot inside. He would have to tell this man, this Uncle Bryn: it was embarrassing. What would he say? In school you could just put your hand up if you wanted to go for a wee. There was a jolt and they turned up a steep hill.

He plucked up his words.

Ok, said Bryn. Hang on a bit. I can't stop the car here.

There was another steep wrench of a turn and they were climbing again. And then the car was pulling up at the side of the road. He got out, and they were in a lay-by and there were trees. His uncle got out too and the boy thought that maybe he'd got out to make sure he didn't run away. But where would he go?

Just take a look over there, said Bryn, afterwards. They crossed the quiet dark road and looked down.

It had been pitch black when they'd got out of the car but his eyes had got used to it and now he could see a lot more. Looking down below them, in the direction that Bryn was pointing – or what was the big dark shadow shape of Bryn pointing – there were lights, lots of them. There was a moon, too, half hidden behind cloud banks. You could make out a scarf of silver. Down there lights were blinking on the blocks and towers of what looked like a big factory. In daylight it would be clear to him, what he'd seen on that first night; security lights and stacked yards, with beyond that the dock and the coast. He thought he was coming to the country, to this farm Bryn had told him about, so what was all this? Whatever it was it was down there, apart from them. Far away really. The light was brilliant all around the factory or ware-house or whatever it was but the rest of the land was still mostly in darkness, though he was now beginning to make out shapes of buildings and trees further away towards the estuary and the sea. Even now, in the dark, he was getting a feel of it, the lie of the land, and he was breathing in summer smells that were all new to him, of earth and cut grass, the faintness of flowers, meadowsweet maybe, heady elderflower. But he did not know the names of all these, not yet, nor what they looked like.

You should be fast asleep in your bed, said Bryn.

He stood beside the boy, aware of being perched on the edge of the night, the edge of the land, high up above the ordinary world. He reckoned he should have felt exhausted, but he didn't. Anything but. He felt quietly and calmly awake and he felt a kind of pride, a satisfaction, glad to have been able to bring the boy back to this safety. To his roots. Even if the circumstances were tragic. He was a practical man. A farmer had to be practical. And unsentimental. But right now he was conscious of unusual and strong emotions welling up. It was the contradiction, he supposed. The sadness, the sense of waste at Olwen's death; the relief that the lad was going to have a chance now. A new beginning. He was aware of something just a little absurd in the way he was basking in a sense of virtue, even heroism, inappropriate though it was. He stood alongside the boy looking down at the fizziness of lights, at the bulk of shadow. There weren't any words to describe how he felt.

four

Still a few miles to go but it's not that far now, says Bryn.

The boy feels a change inside him. Some of the fear and panic and misery has eased a little and healthy, inevitable curiosity has taken over. He's going to a farm and it's in Wales and he's got three cousins, a girl and two boys, twins, and an aunty called Anna, and he's wondering what they're like and whether they're nice. And he's wondering what the farm will be like. He's vividly awake now, looking around him as the car's headlights sweep over hedges and trees with occasionally a few cottages and once a big church with a tower and the sky paler behind it. And at last the car is climbing again and they turn slowly in through gates and pull up in front of a house with a light on in the porch.

Someone on the outside, someone watching from way up high would see a woman in a dressing gown appear at the door and the boy going in through the door and the woman hugging him. Bryn comes behind carrying the boy's things in plastic bags. Someone watching, someone who knew the kind of life the boy had lived before, would think this will be much better for him, the life he'll have here. Not on a deprived inner-city estate with a drunken, depressed mother and a succession of dubious boyfriends. Half fed half the time. Sometimes ignored, sometimes shouted at. It would be easy, it would be obvious to say how much better it will be for him here. And it will be.

But it is not what he knows.

And Bonnie. He loves Bonnie. Bonnie his mother who does not like him to call her anything but Bonnie. And sometimes it's more him looking after her than the other way round.

But she is not always drunk. She is not always shouting. Sometimes she is funny. And kind. And one time they make toffee in a big tin, lovely sticky loads of it. And he drops little hot brown globules of it into cold water to test it. And then they pour it into a tray and wait for it to set and smash it along the lines with the back of a big spoon and eat it, the jaggedy lovely bits of it. It is not all bad: life with Bonnie. Sometimes she tells him stories about animals. About badgers in the woods. About foxes on the mountain. Sometimes she tells him a special spooky story about the holly king.

If that someone on the outside was watching, and had always been watching, that someone could tell you that this moongrey farm is where she came from. Celynnen. And the holly trees are special here, have been allowed to grow tall, pale-boled giants of holly trees. Some grow in a tight cluster, a windbreak for the mountain sheep. Others make the finest, most impenetrable boundary hedge. But in one place, on the track up to Hafod and Ffynnon Wna they grow to form a connecting canopy overhead. And the wind whistles in the spiny leaves.

When she lived here her name wasn't Bonnie but Olwen. Eleven years ago, nearly, when she left this world behind. She would have followed her pied piper of a blues guitarist across the world if need be, if he'd wanted her. She didn't want to be Olwen any more. Too much the name of a farmer's daughter. Too Welsh. Not now that she was going to be cosmopolitan, a city creature. But it wasn't just Danny she was running to. Or running with. She was running away as well. So Danny Walsh was almost an excuse. Not that she knew. Not that she would have believed you if you'd told her. Sometimes we don't know why we do the things we do. The desperate things that can save us, maybe.

five

When Kieran's landlord asked me to clear the flat I found this big leather portfolio propped up at the back of the wardrobe. There were loads of his preliminary sketches in it and some finished paintings too, done in different styles and I should think maybe with long gaps in between as if he was learning as he went along. There were two portraits of a girl with long dark hair, one of her in jeans and a t-shirt, the other with her in a long white and gold dress looking like a Galadriel type from *The Lord of the Rings*. Just for a moment I surprised myself with a stab of jealousy. Whoever she was, I think Kieran must have been in love with her. That comes through with every line, with every single brushstroke.

There were two large brown envelopes as well. One was full of writing, some typed out, some handwritten. Not for the first time I was disappointed in Kieran's handwriting. When you think how well he could draw, well, you'd expect his writing to be beautiful. Now I did see some calligraphy work he'd done once and that was different, special. His ordinary handwriting, though, was kind of ugly really, a mixture of rounded and spiky letters that didn't go together. I wonder now if that was because early on he maybe didn't go to school much and his writing didn't develop properly.

There were some bits of poetry. Some had been crossed out a lot and were pretty scribbly to start with. Among all this stuff, and I've got to be honest straightaway and say Kieran was a much better artist than he was a poet, I found this verse. Just eight lines. When I read them I knew they were Kieran's own. Authentic. That was one of his favourite words, and if he

ever described someone as inauthentic, well, you knew what
he thought of them.

> Someone has nailed some nesting boxes
> on the trees along the lane
> Someone who likes birds enough
> to give them homes for free
> Someone should build houses
> for people sleeping rough tonight
> Someone should have told me
> what it costs to stay naive.

Now Kieran wasn't naive at all, but I think I know what he's
getting at. He means you've got to try really hard not to be
bitter and cynical. That you've got to encourage your own
trust and openness to grow because it's infectious. It spreads.
Trust breeds trust, that kind of thing. Even if bad things have
happened to you, you've got to live your life as if you don't
expect things always to be bad as a matter of course. That it's
not inevitable. He doesn't mean being stupid and soppy. He
means basically giving people a chance. Taking them as you
find. But what does he mean by saying 'someone should have
told me what it costs?' There's a lot of pain there, I think,
though he never showed anyone he was hurting.

I'm sitting on the bed in his room and I'm feeling sad and
at the same time comforted in a way I can't explain because
just a few minutes ago I had this sensation I'll never forget
as long as I live. One of those gorgeous little owls has like a
miracle flown out of his painting and has perched on my
shoulder and told me... told me what? That Kieran, or his
spirit, is still around? Did it really happen? Did I imagine it?

I don't know how long I sit there. It's getting dark but I

don't want to get up and put the light on. I want to keep this twilight, holding on to this feeling that I know is probably wishful thinking, no matter how strong and real it seems, hold on a bit longer to Kieran's words, and it's as if I can hear his voice speaking them.

Eventually I do get up and put the light on. In the second envelope I find drawings but they seem to be children's drawings this time. There's one of a road snaking up a hill though most of it is out of sight, hidden under a tunnel of trees growing over the road, and the trees have dark green shiny leaves. There's one with a strange figure at the end of the road, where the trees change and spread out, made with a firm outline in black but the middle of the figure is bright yellow and red as if it's on fire, even his face, though you can just about make out the features. Then there's a different tree with a broad trunk, and on one branch there's a big cartoon snake with its pointed tongue sticking out. Some of the other pictures seem to be about the same thing but an older child has drawn these. They're much better drawn but perhaps they've lost a bit of their power somehow, as if the energy's gone into how the drawing's made instead of getting over what it's actually about. But what is it about? There's something else in the envelope, a school exercise book with the name Kieran Walsh. Walsh? I have this awful feeling that there's a secret here that I don't want to know, because my Kieran is Kieran Wood. And this is his school book. I know that for sure and it's important or he wouldn't have kept it all this time. He decided to change his name though. Why?

six

Bryn is sitting at the kitchen table doing his VAT returns. This is a task he usually puts off but he's actually glad to do it this time, anything to take his mind off other things. Arrangements for the funeral can get going now, anyway, since the results of the post mortem have shown it was an accident. Thank God for that, Bryn thinks with a shudder, not so much on Olwen's behalf as the boy's. All this will be hard enough for him to deal with as it is, but imagine what it would have been like for him if it had turned out she'd been murdered? No one had pushed her down the stairs, anyway, and that was something, but fancy coming home from school and finding your mother like that. It was something you'd never forget.

Thinking about Olwen brings it all back. The reasons why she left, the trouble with his mother, Betty. All those feelings of incredulous envy which he's never really come to terms with, the way his mother and Olwen saw, felt, and simply knew things about this place that he just didn't, the way they had an understanding of it all that was beyond him. And he loved it at least as much as they did. More. Just look at the way Olwen couldn't get away fast enough. He knew he was being unfair, that it was much more complicated than that: that Olwen's need to leave Celynnen behind was as much to do with love as hate. She'd had a connection with the land that he couldn't even begin to imagine. And then there was that Danny Walsh. Bryn remembers his slippery charm with a sudden rush of anger that leaves an acid taste in his mouth. So where's that bastard now, eh? he asks himself. When his poor little scrap of a son needs him? But what good would he be anyway, even if he were still around? Bryn knows that he is now the nearest thing the lad will ever have to a father.

There's a movement in the yard and he looks out, seeing that Mari's back with the boy. She'd been taking him on a conducted tour of the mountain, sat up high on Minstrel the pony's back while she led him on the rein. The boy was pleased as punch. He waved happily at his uncle now, carrying the saddle to hang up by the door in the old wash house. Pity his own boys were too old to be friends for him really, but let's face it, they'd be thirteen in October, and four years apart at that age is light years different. To Sion and Huw, Kieran was just a little kid, and anyway being twins they were used to being tied up so much with each other. Still, Anna'd impressed upon them that they should try to involve Kieran in what they were doing but the boy had his own ideas, it seemed. He just liked mooching about on his own.

He looks half starved, Bryn thinks, guiltily uncomfortable with the idea since it reflects so poorly on Olwen. By all accounts her drinking bouts had reached epic proportions. She would never have been cruel to the child, he consoles himself, not deliberately, not directly cruel, though as he'd long since had no dealings whatsoever with his sister he couldn't be confident even of that. There was no getting round it: Olwen was an alcoholic who neglected her child. Mrs McFadden had said there was scarcely anything to eat in the house. In the fridge there'd been just a couple of yoghurts and half a carton of eggs well past their sell-by. The boy had been a regular at the local takeaway for his favourite chips and curry sauce when he was able to get his hands on some money. It was obvious what Olwen's priority would be.

He heard the door go and Mari came in.

Where is he now? asked Bryn.

He's gone out the back again, said Mari. He's got loads of energy, dad, and it's all a big adventure for him. Stop worrying about him all the time.

Exploring, that's what he was doing. Finding out everything he could about this new world. He was used to his own company. He'd always made sure kids didn't come back to his place because he never knew what state Bonnie'd be in. Young as he was, he knew that a mother who remained unwashed and still in her dressing gown at teatime, among empty cans and chaos was not one to be proud of. In his way he was trying to protect her, too. He might have lived all his life in a succession of tough places but he wasn't exactly streetwise because he'd never mixed enough with other kids to know the score. Yet in so many ways he was old for his years. He had acquired a sixth sense, a condensed child wisdom all his own. It taught him to keep to himself.

He developed a reticence that was close to secrecy, learning to be both practical and enterprising, often doing their meagre shopping, taking bedding to the launderette when it became obvious Bonnie wasn't going to get round to it, and generally keeping the place going. He didn't think of this as unusual, it was just the way things were. Mrs McFadden next door was always there to help out if he got really stuck. She came in sometimes when Bonnie was sleeping after one of her binges, and they made a conspiratorial game of it. She lent him money too, when all the fifty pence pieces in the green teapot were gone, when Bonnie's coat pockets were empty and there wasn't even a penny to be found deep down between the cushions and the frames of the chairs. Mrs McFadden was kind but she called him her 'grand little man' which made him squirm. Still, it was good to have someone like her around. After the ambulance had come to get Bonnie, and when it seemed to him they were all pretending to him that she was still alive when he knew quite well she was dead, Mrs McFadden had stayed with him in the house. She'd known that Bonnie came from a farm in Wales, knew that somewhere there were letters with an address and a phone number. She'd found them eventually. Bonnie might never have replied to those letters and it must have been ages ago since she'd received them, but she'd kept them, hadn't she? That had to mean something, though he couldn't for the life of him understand why anyone would ever leave a place like this. He would never leave Celynnen as long as he lived. Not ever.

When he came back in after his exploring, Aunty Anna would ask him where he'd been and what he'd been doing and he was happy to tell her. Except for one thing. He wasn't going to tell anyone about the holly king.

It wasn't that he thought perhaps no one would believe him. He was quite sure no one would believe him. No, it was more worrying than that. He was afraid that he didn't quite believe what had happened himself. He'd had to push thoughts of the holly king out of his head, and stop trying to ask himself what exactly he'd seen that morning, what had actually happened. He had no idea. Perhaps he'd imagined it. Anyway, to make sure he didn't see him again, not if he could help it, he stopped going to the top of the holly hill and running down it so fast he almost flew. Before long he'd stopped going in that direction altogether.

There was so much to explore, though he did feel a peculiar sort of guilt to begin with. He was happy. And with Bonnie dead he was sure he shouldn't have been feeling happy at all.

It was like letting Bonnie down. Soon though, almost without noticing to start with, he began to feel that Bonnie was there with him, not the adult Bonnie who'd been his mother, but the child called Olwen, who it seemed to him, more and more, had never really left this magical place after all.

He felt that he was constantly walking in her footsteps. The places he found that spoke so clearly to him were surely her places, places she'd loved, and played in and dreamed in. He didn't put all this into words in his head; it wasn't like these were thoughts at all, and there was no explaining it, but he did keep getting odd tingling feelings of newness and familiarity combined.

When he was sitting by the pond, in the hollow of the field behind the farm, it was almost as if his hands were her hands. It was an activation of memory, but it wasn't his memory. He plucked a handful of stiff mares' tails that grew in the pond's gooey margin of mud and silt and he pulled the serrated sections of the stems apart. What a peculiar plant this was. As he set the separate sections down in lines, in graduated order of size, he felt smaller freckled hands were animating his. Perhaps to begin with this scared him, but he soon got used to it, even welcomed it. Prudently though, just as he'd told no one about the holly king, he also kept all this to himself. What he didn't know was that he wasn't the only one to keep a secret.

seven

You could say he's in denial. Or that he's lacking insight into his own condition. There again, you could say quite simply that he's been keeping a secret from himself all this time.

It's out now. There's something in the boy's gestures, expressions that's painful to see. His features may be Danny's but the way he moves, speaks, laughs, that's entirely Olwen. Bryn can see and feel now what he couldn't, or wouldn't, admit to before. That he was always jealous of Olwen, even when he was just a kid. He'd wanted a brother, was very disappointed when a baby girl turned up. Still, aged no more than three and a half, he soon becomes fascinated by this little brother substitute. And the feeling's reciprocated. As soon as she can toddle round after him Olwen dogs his heels. She looks up to him. Big brother. Hero, even. He's quite flattered really. Quite proud. But she does get in the way sometimes. Like on that day of the shearing. He's eight, nine years old. The same age as Kieran is now. He wants to do men's work. Join in. Be with his father and the shearers and the lads from Nant Coch. It's time he was taken seriously. But Olwen is yelling and mythering. She wants to come too.

Just take her up there with you for a while, his mother says. Let her see what's going on. She'll soon have had enough of it.

Far from becoming quickly bored with it all, Olwen's entranced with the noise and the bustle. Who wouldn't be? All that vivid action of sheep and men and dogs. All that clamour and commotion. Together they stand by the sycamore tree that grows out of the tumbledown stones of Hafod. The light is in the tree, breathing and flickering. It feels like there's thousands of bewildered sheep up there. The sound of their bleating reverberates all around, only now it's more a great chorale of something akin to bellowing. They watch as the men take hold of the sheep in their strong arms, their capable hands. Briefly Olwen cries. She thinks they're hurting the sheep. Reassured by her big brother she watches a demonstration of what looks so easy and so casual but isn't. She watches as the fleeces pile up on the floor of the truck in soft, sad, smudged, magnificent piles. And then the sheep are pushing out through the hurdles, scrawny and vulnerable on their suddenly-too-thin legs, shrugging their strange light shoulders. And the panic is still in them, their tumult a thing that's all around them rather than just a sound, tangible in the smell and the pace of them as they scramble and run, up and out and back to the bare tops.

Bryn's resentful. He wants to be in the middle of all this, part of it, not just a bystander with a little sister in tow. It's time for a bit of bribery and corruption. Promising her ice-cream when she gets home, he grabs Olwen's hand and they take a short cut down the steep slope by Ffynnon Wna. And here he finds out for the first time that Olwen is different, that she can see things he can't see.

Look at the ponies, she yells with delight, clapping her hands with uncontained excitement. She tugs at his sleeve. Bryn, she shouts. I want to go up there. Look, look.

No, he says sternly, staring into her face, her eyes, to make quite sure. This isn't a game. This is real. Quite genuine. What is she seeing?

He's tugging her along quite fiercely now. She's yelling all the way home, still complaining when they finally come in through the back door, snivelling loudly, wiping her snotty nose on her sleeve.

Bryn wouldn't let me see the ponies, she whines, hardly able to tear the words out in the middle of all her choking and gulping.

What ponies? their mother asks, wiping her watering eyes with the corner of her apron as she chops onions for the stew tonight.

It was by Ffynnon Wna, says Bryn, his exasperation making him hoarse. She said there were these ponies but she's making it up. There weren't any there.

And now he's slamming the door behind him and setting off back up there to the shearing, knowing that on some level quite closed to him those ponies were there and were real. Knowing too that he has to get out of there before he sees the expression on his mother's face. He has an idea he knows what it will be. There's a mystery here that he has no inkling of but somehow, even now, he's able to recognise that whatever it is, this is just the beginning. And he's excluded from it.

eight

On the inside cover of the school exercise book that gave me such a shock and made me think he must have had some deep dark secret he was determined to hide, I found this, written in big ugly letters:

Kieran Walsh
Celynnen

Foel Gron
Flintshire
Wales
UK
Europe
The Northern Hemisphere
Earth
The Solar System
The Milky Way
The Universe

I suppose every kid writes out their own version of that at some time. It's important. Even awesome. It means that kid has made the discovery that he's just a little speck in the middle of vast space. Quite scary. But by thinking it out, where he actually is in the middle of everything and writing it down, starting with the house he lives in and placing it in its surroundings and then bit by bit moving outwards as if he's creating loads and loads of concentric circles until he's mapped the whole cosmos right there on that piece of paper in front of him, well, by then he's proved to himself how amazing and simply unimaginably huge it all is while at the same time controlling it all, in a way. He is, after all, at the centre of his own universe. So is everybody else. That's an extraordinary thing. I think of Kieran aged nine years old. His mother's dead and he's come to live with his aunty and uncle and his three cousins on this farm in Wales. Later, when I go there myself, I'll find that in the village there's a little grey stone cottage where his granny lives. Only he calls her Nain. On the very first day his Aunty Anna takes him there (even then I think there's maybe trouble with her husband Bryn over this) he goes out into the garden at the back and sees this amazing bird he thinks is a parrot. He rushes in and tells them. You've seen the green woodpecker, his Nain says. The yaffle some call him. Or the rain bird. He was there this morning by the hedge looking for ants.

It's become so clear to me, this picture in my head of the young Kieran in his bewildering new world. And this little lad grows up to be the most remarkable person I've ever known and I want to cry. At the sheer unfairness of things.

When I hear politicians going on about 'family values' I want to puke, quite honestly. That's because of my own experience, but hell, scratch the surface of any supposedly happy family and you'll find plenty that isn't happy at all. It's a cynical lie. But these people were all doing their very best. They wanted so much to make his life better. I think about this and then I realise, of course, Kieran knew they loved him. Every day they made that clear to him in everything they did. He knew they had their differences and very strong disagreements about the way things should be, but he knew too that all these differences grew out of the fact that they cared. And I wonder then if things are actually meant to happen the way they do. That there is maybe a kind of fate or destiny at the back of it all. And for the umpteenth time I wish Kieran was here and I could ask him what he thought. Weirdly, I even wonder if what he thought when he was alive would be different from what he thinks now he's dead. Stop it, I tell myself. You're not making sense.

Efforts were made to find out if Kieran had any relatives. Not by me. It was Jon and Vanda at the Yoga Centre sorted all that out, like they sorted the funeral. They'd known him longer than anybody, years longer than me. Because he had his consultations at the centre I suppose they had official things, like contracts and receipts, maybe, stuff like that.

Anyway, there was nothing to show there were any family connections at all. And now I'd found this.

The first thing I did was get hold of the telephone book to look up all the Walshes and all the Woods in the Foel Gron area. Nothing doing. But already I'm beginning to feel that this is my quest. I knew it was a long shot. Ridiculous really. Kieran's twenty-ninth birthday had been last month. How long ago had he written this? And even if he had lived in this Celynnen place it might only have been for a short time and there might be no link at all with anybody living there now. That was the sensible, rational stuff I was thinking. Stronger than that though was this feeling I had that I ought to try at least to find out if there was some connection. In my bones I felt there was.

I made a last search of the wardrobe. Half disappearing between the floor and the back I found two photographs. In the first there were three boys, two in their early teens wearing Man Utd replica shirts and one, younger, and with dark hair, wearing an Everton shirt. He was playing keepy-uppy with a football and his movement made the photo blurred, but I think it was Kieran. In the second snap he was there again, this time with an older girl, standing by a stable door. He was holding out his hand with something in it for this brown horse that was nuzzling his hand, tickling him I should think, by the way he was laughing. Everyone in these photographs was relaxed and happy looking. I got everything together: the paintings, the typed and the handwritten material, the lot, and I went round to Jon and Vanda's with it.

She was taking one of her Pilates classes but Jon was there. He was really interested in all these things, spreading everything out on the table. I told him I thought I should try to find this Celynnen and get in touch with the people there now, see if they knew anything. Like me he thought they might be Kieran's relatives, and he seemed keen. When Vanda arrived he changed his tune. She was hostile to the idea from the start.

Hasn't it occurred to you that if Kieran changed his name and had nothing to do with his family there's probably a good reason? she said, in that sneery, condescending tone she has sometimes. I'd leave well alone, she said.

I looked at Jon in the hope he might say something different but his expression was blank, detached. I'd always known who wore the trousers there, though, hadn't I?

Next stop was the library. I found a very detailed map that showed at least some of the farms and the bigger houses standing on their own in the country, but there was no Celynnen. Still, there was the village of Foel Gron, which was a start. It was in the middle of nowhere and I didn't think there was likely to be much of a bus service, but then, just by a fluke, I heard Jon say something about going with Vanda on Saturday to see an exhibition of ceramics some friend of theirs had got on in this gallery in Cheshire somewhere. It would've meant them going in a roundabout way admittedly, but couldn't they drop me off in Foel Gron so I could look for Celynnen, and then pick me up on the way back? Vanda was pretty begrudging but I reckon she'd caught some of my curiosity herself by now. So it was settled. I just couldn't wait till Saturday.

The day dawned frosty and bright with a sharp blue sky. I couldn't wait to get there and though it couldn't have been more than twenty miles away, or thereabouts, it was a different world. There was no shop or post office in the village where I could enquire, but the one pub, The Black Lion, was just opening as we arrived. They gave us directions to a farm we'd find on the left, up a steep lane that started at the back of the church. I was expecting holly trees so didn't realise we'd got there till I saw Celynnen clearly marked on the gate of what seemed to be an ordinary-looking and quite small farm house set in a slight dip in the land.

Jon and Vanda were going to wait while I went to see if there was anyone at home. When I opened the heavy gate and walked across the yard I saw that round the side of the house a track set off up the hill again, very steeply now, and that here at last was the tunnel of holly. I waved to Jon and Vanda and gave them a thumbs-up sign, but they didn't turn to go till I'd knocked at the door just as it opened. I asked the man standing there if he knew someone called Kieran Walsh. He looked a bit awkward so I was glad when a woman appeared behind him. I liked her smile. And I was thrilled I'd found the right place. There was no mistaking it, but how strangely blank and empty the track and the trees looked, just for a moment, without the weird figure in Kieran's painting. Not that I'd expected to see it, of course, but still, I wanted that vivid flare of flame, the dark-edged brightness that hurt your eyes. Kieran's picture was misleading anyway, in that what you could call the tunnel, the part where the branches entangled overhead, only extended for a short distance. After that, winding further and higher up the hill again, it was just a holly hedge growing on both sides, the trees in it quite tall and still impressive but not meeting over the road. To a child the tunnel part must have made the most impact, along with the sudden, drop-of-a-curtain darkness as you walked inside.

nine

Why did this girl have to turn up from nowhere, stirring up trouble, opening old wounds?

He'd been crossing the landing when he saw her through the window, coming over the yard as if to the front door but then she turned to the side of the house. What on earth did she want? By the time he'd got downstairs and was just about to open the door she must have come round to the front again. They startled each other. Nonplussed and blushing with awkwardness, she fumbled for words. I'm sorry to bother you like this, she said. I wonder, do you happen to have known someone called Kieran Walsh?

By this time Anna had appeared behind him. You'd better come in, said Bryn.

If they'd had any warning they could have lit the fire in the parlour. It was too cold to take the girl in there.

Come through to the kitchen, said Anna, and Bryn was aware, yet again, of his wife's graciousness, how she put people at ease so quickly. In no time she'd got the kettle on and was introducing the girl to Mari, who was going shopping to Chester and had brought Carys for them to mind while she was gone. The girl showed them an old school exercise book. Yes, it was Kieran's, no doubt about that, Ysgol Foel Gron printed on the cover, and on the inside, in the boy's ungainly writing, their address. Despite himself, Bryn felt himself well up. So many mixed emotions, so much unresolved sadness and regret.

There were paintings, drawings, photographs. Would you believe, that's me and Minstrel, said Mari. Dad, d'you remember, early on, that day I took him over the mountain, all round? He couldn't get enough of it all. It was like he was in heaven... then she paused, realising what she'd said.

Well, he is now, said Anna. Then slowly, heavily, to think of someone murdering him. That's terrible.

The girl told them that Kieran had become an urban shaman. Bryn raised his eyebrows, looking covertly at his wife and making no comment. He was, by all accounts, an artist of some repute. Painted people's totems, apparently. Whatever that meant.

There was a long pause. Anna picked up the first painting of the tunnel of holly and the strange figure standing near the oak tree, the snake on the lowest branch.

I remember this picture, Anna said, then, as she looked at the other drawings and paintings she realised it was the same scene, the same mysterious person. He's drawn this again and again, she said, her voice shrunk to a whisper. And painted it in different ways. Then, very quietly, she went on. When he first arrived he would go to the top of the hill and run down it so fast we were afraid he'd fall. It was a kind of compulsion. There was a social worker involved in the beginning, and briefly a child psychiatrist. She said to let him be: that he'd grow out of it, and that even if he did fall, it wouldn't be the end of the world. That perhaps he needed to do it, work off all his pent-up feelings. That it might be something to do with the trauma...

Unspoken was the obvious question. Why did he keep coming back to this picture? Why the obsession with this puzzling, bizarre figure, seemingly out of myth or fairy tale? Even more crucially, why had Kieran left so suddenly? He had written to them, apparently, thanking them for everything, saying simply that he had to go. Then there was the matter of why he'd changed his name.

So many undercurrents in the warm, comfortably cluttered room, the shifting fire making crackling sounds, the baby sitting on Mari's knee, crooning softly to herself as if to catch the rhythms of the plunging fire, tugging at the ears of her toy panda one minute, poking gently with her chubby fingers at her mother's nose and mouth the next. All so peaceful, you might think, and then Anna stood up abruptly. We'll have to tell Betty, she said and the reverie, however superficial it might have been, was shattered. Look Mari, she said. You get off now. Come on, leave Carys with me and we'll go down to Betty's now.

She turned to the girl. Could you come? she asked. Betty would like to hear it from you. It would mean more coming from you. About his life and what he did, she paused, struggling, and how he changed people's lives.

He saved my life, the girl said. Definitely. I really owe him.

I'm not sure about this, said Bryn. Not at all. I don't think it's a good idea. But mother and daughter alike were adamant. I'll come too, said Mari. I can go to Chester anytime.

Bryn was on his feet, the energy coming off him like smoke. It was as if something long unresolved was warring in him, a conflict so fundamental that his whole body burned with it. The girl felt this. Of course people could respond to what they called, for want of a better name, the atmosphere in a room, to a sense of tension, unvoiced antagonism, things like that. She'd never felt anything like this, this degree of intensity, and it frightened her.

Have it your own way, he said. And then he was gone. He didn't exactly slam the door after him. It might have been better if he had. Instead, he closed it very softly.

Anna banked up the logs and put the fireguard in place. Seeing the girl's concern, she reassured her. He'll be alright, she said. It's good that we know now. It's a relief. And Kieran obviously had good years. Made a difference. You can't imagine... you'd think it would hurt less with time passing. But it doesn't. As an afterthought she added, Bryn was very close to Kieran. Felt very responsible for him.

That was the trouble really, Mari cut in. Too many people feeling too much responsibility, so that in the end I think Kieran felt responsible for all this responsibility people felt towards him. Does that sound daft?

Not a bit, the girl said.

Bryn watched them cross the yard. He watched them get into the car and set off down the road to his mother's in the village. When they'd gone he whistled for Meg and the collie came running, jumping up into the back of the Land Rover, wagging her tail. He drove up through the tunnel of holly, up to the tops, to the ruins of Hafod, and to Ffynon Wna, to check on the sheep, to walk on the mountain on his own as he so often did, thinking about everything. About his mother, and their slow burning feud, patched up in recent years, maybe, but wouldn't all this put a bomb under everything all over again?

He thought about Olwen and he thought about Kieran. What a mess it had all been. And it shouldn't have been like that. Yes, reluctantly he understood why the lad had had enough of them all. Why he had to go. But it still rankled. It still caused pain. The mystery of what had happened to Kieran was solved anyway. At least they knew now.

ten

Bryn remembered how, from the word go, he had this strong feeling that Kieran shared Olwen's talent for, well, whatever it was. He still didn't know how to describe it, a kind of clairvoyance, maybe? The ability to see things that weren't there, or were no longer there, anyway. Echoes, if you like. He'd never decided on a word for it because that would have made it real and he couldn't have coped with that. He had no evidence whatsoever that Kieran possessed this gift, or, more accurately perhaps, curse, not until the day he took him up to the tops, to Ffynon Wna, to show him the view.

Stubbornly, determinedly, he'd tried to discount his hunch about Kieran, telling himself that the boy was a townie through and through, and therefore hardly likely to react to his surroundings in the way Olwen had. There was no getting round the fact that, townie or not, Kieran's delight in his new environment was extraordinary. Right from the start. It was like a total surrender to the land. Fanciful way of putting it but nonetheless true. The lad had taken to the fields and the copses and the strange bushy, humpy texture of the mountain as if he'd lived in the midst of it all his life.

Kieran thought it was very odd to call it a mountain. It wasn't a mountain, surely, not what he thought of as a mountain. But once you got away from the greenness and the smoothness immediately surrounding the farm the land changed colour and appearance, became shaggier and wilder and browner. And there was gorse everywhere. This was what they called the mountain. It certainly got steeper but not in the jagged way you'd expect. It was suddenly thoroughly pitted and uneven, full of hollows and hummocks, tufted with reeds and tussocky grasses or straggly with bits of bracken and briars. Not that he knew these names then.

It was quiet and still on the day he went up to the tops with Bryn for the first time, but generally it must have been windy up there because all these funny little trees leaned over all one way and sheep wandered in and out of these little clumps of trees that were like wild gardens. These were hawthorns and rowans and there were the occasional silver birches, too, the ones he liked best of all, but on that first day they were just magical growing things. He'd not learned any labels to put on them.

It was hot and it was shimmery and he was looking up to the highest part of the mountain when he saw a group of men on the horizon. It was t-shirt weather, definitely, but these men were wearing jerkins and caps and peculiar looking trousers. Most of them seemed to be carrying things over their shoulders, and they'd appeared out of nowhere, talking about something, in a very bothered about it sort of way, arguing maybe. Then one of them seemed to burst out laughing, tilting back his head, and then they were all laughing, starting to move together down the slope towards them. Kieran felt there was something a bit worrying about them, though he couldn't tell you what it was.

What are all those men doing there? he asked his uncle. Bryn seemed awkward and somehow embarrassed, and Kieran noticed he didn't look in the men's direction at all.

I can't see any men, Bryn said, and he was moving very fast now, the boy struggling to keep up with him. Kieran deliberately didn't look round for a few minutes (it seemed a much longer time than a few minutes but it couldn't have been any longer than that) but when he did, sort of sideways, trying as hard as he could not to even move his head if he could help it, he saw that the men weren't there anymore. He wanted to say to Bryn something like: it's alright now. They've gone now. But something else told him not to.

Later, Bryn asked himself whether Kieran had seen the men after enquiring about the unevenness of the ground, and after he'd told him about the miners. No. He knew for sure that the boy had seen his invisible men on the horizon a good while before asking about the hummocks and hollows. So it wasn't as if his own words had put the idea in the boy's head. He'd seen the lead miners of old before knowing they'd ever existed, before he knew anything about the mountain's mining history. It had confirmed his theory, anyway, and he wished it hadn't. Like mother, like son. Well, God help the lad. How on earth was he supposed to respond? He still had no idea. With Olwen, Bryn had blocked it all out, pretended with her, and privately, with himself, that she was just making things up, even as he knew she wasn't. As she grew into the charismatic, vulnerable teenager she was to become he persisted in maintaining his apparent disbelief. Now, however unhelpful that reaction might have been, he couldn't think of a better one. His first impulse, naturally, was to protect the boy from his own abilities. How?

Then Kieran had come running up behind him, and had asked him the question. He answered him, self-consciously. It's all humpy and bumpy like this because a hundred years ago, and a lot longer ago than that when it all started, this whole area was covered with little mines. People came up from the towns and started to dig, looking for lead mostly, and wherever they dug they left holes and heaps behind them. It took years and years but eventually the lead ran out. And then it took a good while for nature to take over again. The holes and heaps are still there, though, but disguised.

And you've got to be careful, even now. Most of the old mine-shafts have been capped and fenced off but just occasionally someone falls down one that's never been mapped, so they didn't even know it was there. And even without the mine-shafts to consider, the mountain can still be dangerous because it's so uneven underfoot. You could easily twist your ankle or break it, and end up lying there all night. And if it was winter you'd freeze to death, simple as that.

The boy shuddered then, Bryn remembered. He'd hoped at the time that this cautionary tale would give him a proper respect for the mountain. Take his mind off the sight of ghostly miners too for a while. Nowadays of course you wouldn't have to lie there in the cold and die of hypothermia. You'd have your mobile phone with you, but when Kieran came to Celynnen mobile phones hadn't even been thought of. Or had they? Bryn wasn't sure. Perhaps a few yuppies in London had them, great stonking things as long as your face.

Now, having just heard of Kieran's death, shaken, sad-dened, but glad and frankly astonished to hear that he'd found some productive outlet for his talents, Bryn was walk-ing again on the mountain, remembering the boy's eagerness, regretting their estrangement. An urban shaman, eh? What the hell did an urban shaman do?

Reluctantly he remembered something that had happened long ago, something he'd experienced and denied almost in the same breath. It made him acutely uncomfortable now to even think about it and he certainly hadn't intentionally recalled it to mind. It had resurfaced of its own accord, the only occasion in his entire life that he'd had just an inkling of what it was like to be an Olwen or a Kieran.

It was only a few weeks after Kieran had come to live with them. Anna had asked him to call the lad in for his tea. It was the school holidays and Huw and Sion had gone off some-where with a couple of friends. Mari was there, he knew. He'd been crossing the yard when Anna'd banged on the window. Tell Kieran tea's ready, she shouted. Bryn reckoned he'd be down by the pond. And he was. Bryn remembered the air was gauzy with midges. The pond had been bigger then. All the hot summers in between had dried it up considerably but in those days, twenty years ago, there'd been a wide shallow margin and that's where Kieran was sitting as he so often did. Bryn was just about to call down to him when he saw some-thing strange.

For a moment it was as if there were two children playing there. He blinked. It had to be a trick of the light. No, there were definitely two of them. And he knew who the other one was. He shouted now, and Kieran turned towards his voice. As he did so it was as if the other child faded. There was an outline for a quivering few seconds and then it was gone.

eleven

Sometimes an absence can mean more than a presence. Sometimes someone who isn't there can dominate those who are. Bryn wasn't with us in Betty's kitchen (I like these women whose lives revolve around their kitchens) but it felt as if he was. In the car, on the way down to the village to Betty's tiny, end-of-terrace cottage, Anna told me there'd been bad feeling between mother and son off and on for a long time, and that

I shouldn't upset myself about it because that was just how it was.

I'd got the impression by now that everything would be explained and that when it was, I'd understand why Kieran had to leave. I also remembered Vanda's warning, when she insisted in her superior way that he must have turned his back on his family for a good reason and that I should keep out of it. Now though, I couldn't help wondering if I'd done the right thing in coming here at all, even if Anna did keep stressing that, from their point of view, it was better to know what had happened than to be kept in the dark. Anyway, by the time I was sitting in the front of the car, with Anna driving, and Mari and the baby in the back, I'd got this awful feeling of dread. To tell the truth if I could have pressed a magic button and whisked myself back in time to just before setting off with Jon and Vanda this morning that's exactly what I'd have done. Too late now, though. Me and my quest. I'd been so determined, hadn't I? I was caught up in all this whether I liked it or not and I was worried sick that the old lady we were going to see would be really cut up when she heard what had happened to Kieran.

Betty might have been bent and frail, in her eighties at least, but she was bright and clear-eyed and very clear-minded. Of course she was shocked to hear how he'd died but she seemed relieved to hear that Kieran had made a life for himself, that people loved him, and appreciated the things he could do. The baby'd fallen asleep by now and as we sat in the snug small room we spoke very quietly so as not to wake her. Four generations of the women in Bryn's family but he wasn't there. It seems right, though, that in the picture I still retain so clearly of them, I can see him in that room with us. Just goes to show how your memory can play tricks on you. We were never all together at all, and that was the one and only day I'd ever see them.

I found the words to say I was sorry I'd caused difficulties with Bryn, thinking of how he'd stormed out of the room. I mightn't have known then what it was all about, but I knew for sure that I'd opened a can of worms and I wished to God I hadn't. Betty was looking through Kieran's pictures by now, and at the exercise book and the scribbly poems, including the one about putting up the nesting boxes for the birds.

Bryn put one up for bluetits in the back here, she says. They nest in it every spring. She looks at me. You mustn't think we're enemies, or that he hates me. It's not like that.

D'you remember the green woodpecker? Anna asked.

Betty nodded. He loved birds, Kieran, she said. But his favourite was always the green woodpecker. That first time he came here and thought he'd seen a parrot.... She chuckled then, but as she did so, the sound changed in her throat. Her shoulders started to shake as she tried to get a grip on herself and Anna got up from her chair.

It's alright, Betty, Anna said, but the old lady didn't want to be comforted. I caused so much trouble, she said. As Anna started to speak she lifted her hand to stop her. No, Anna. It's true. It's got to be said. Time passes but it doesn't change anything. Then she turned from Anna to look at me. Has she told you what happened? she asked.

Anna was half kneeling in front of Betty's chair now, holding the old lady's hand. I thought that was up to you, she said. I didn't know whether you'd want us to tell her.

She's made the effort to find us, said Betty with new firmness. The least we can do is tell her what happened. And why.

I don't know quite how it starts, really, the order in which, between them, they told the whole story but this is how I remember it, or at least how I've put it all together in my head.

When Betty married Ted, Bryn's father, her own parents hadn't been exactly thrilled. She came from a farm called Maes Derwen, not even three miles away as that proverbial crow flies, but a very different farm from Celynnen. It was a large prosperous lowland farm. Still is, said Betty. They've got a famous herd of beef cattle. They do some dairy, mind, and they grow a lot of wheat. It's a very different set up from a small hill farm with just sheep. There's always been a grazier tradition on the mountain, you see. It's unusual, very much so nowadays, because it's mostly common land. Celynnen doesn't have much land of its own. Very often graziers make ends meet with gardening for people, painting and decorating. Things like that. Actually, Bryn can turn his hand to anything, he's very practical. Of course in the past it would be a bit of mining for lead, maybe. As an extra. Long ago.

Here she paused and looked at Anna, but it was Mari who cut in.

Can I tell it, Nain? she asked, and the old lady nodded with a weariness that made me want to disappear. Anna wasn't comfortable either, the strain showing on her face.

I didn't know much about, well, the background to all this until the summer before I left for college to do my teacher's training, said Mari. It was a terrible time because Kieran was ill and it brought a lot of simmering things to the boil. Nain had taken him to Maes Derwen to see the skull in the chimney...

Looking at me Anna bridled. She must have seen a look of surprise cross my face, but she'd read it wrongly. I'd remembered Kieran telling me about the guardian skulls, as if this was just more general information. When it actually was nothing of the kind. You've got it all back to front, Mari, she said. It sounds awful put like that.

Makes me sound as if I'm off my head, said Betty. Then, sadly, perhaps I was.

No. You thought you were doing the right thing, said Anna. The point of all this is that the Vaughans of Maes Derwen have, well, they're part of a tradition, you see. One that goes back much further than the lead mining on the mountain. No one knows how far back. The responsibility would pass from generation to generation, to be the Guardian. Some of the old families round here still know about this, I suppose, but most people have forgotten about it now, and by the time Betty was born it was largely ignored anyway...

Except for my grandfather, said Betty. He tried to revive it. I was the only one who was interested. My father didn't like it. My brothers didn't either. They saw it as old-fashioned, superstitious nonsense. Or worse. With my father so set against it, my grandfather and I kept it a secret, just the two of us, though my mother was aware of it, on some level. She saw her role as keeping the peace. The way Anna does now. It's not a big thing, really. Or it needn't have been. Every month we would walk the bounds. And it wasn't just the Maes Derwen land. It took in the whole area, up on to the mountain as well, including Celynnen, and thereabouts. We didn't make a song and dance about it. It was just a long country walk really. Except for noticing and blessing all the plants and animals in the old way and stopping in the special places like Ffynnon Wna and Craig Rwlff to repeat the rhymes...

Now Mari interrupted again. This is the amazing thing, she said. Even Nain, and her Taid before her, didn't know the relevance of Craig Rwlff. What it means. They just took the name for granted. This is a very anglicised area, you see, though less so now, with Welsh schools and everything. That's made a big difference. What I mean is, it's always been borderland, historically. Offa's dyke. Wat's dyke. All that. So it's as least as much Saxon as Welsh.

Mercian, if we're going to be precise, said Anna. The edge in her voice told me she wanted Mari to let Betty tell her own story in her own way. There was something annoyingly over-eager about Mari, and perhaps unfeeling too, as if she was just excited by the whole thing and unaware of how upsetting it was to the others. Anyway, there was no stopping her.

With a name like Craig Rwlff, you're reminded. It's a kind of language fusion. It's Wolf Rock, really. Sort of Wenglish. In Welsh it would be Craig y Blaidd. Just think how far that name goes back. And at Ffynnon Wna, right up till the First World War, there used to be this tradition of taking all the horses up there to walk them through the well water. The vicar would be there, and he'd scoop up water on to their backs with a special bowl that was kept in the church. It was a Christian festival, of course, and it had been carried out at least since Tudor times, we know that for sure, but some people think it goes right back to the Romano-Celtic goddess, Epona. That's where we get the word pony...

Ok Mari, Anna said. Let Nain tell the story herself. It's Kieran we want to hear about anyway.

Mari looked peeved. It's all relevant, she said.

Betty blew her nose fiercely and sat up straight, composing herself. Part of the Maes Derwen house, she said, her voice stronger again, the oldest part, goes back centuries. No one knows how long really. Long before the Vaughans ever got there, anyway. And, hidden in a chimney breast, there's a skull. This represents the Guardian. She looked at me as she said this, as if I was in some way critical. Very primitive, and very sinister, I suppose, but when my grandfather showed it me I didn't think that, just how privileged we were to have such an ancient thing as this in our home. And in our family. Here she looked up at Anna. For reassurance, I think. You could see how close these two were. Anna was sitting on a straight-backed chair she'd moved from the table and put next to Betty's armchair. Again she took hold of Betty's hand but spoke herself this time. Betty sank back in her chair and looked relieved.

From the word go Kieran liked to spend time with Nain. Mari and the twins were already in High School, and either Bryn or I would take them down to the village to get the school bus. This would be about ten past eight, too early for Kieran to go to Ysgol Foel Gron really, especially as to begin with he was bullied quite a bit. Rather than make two journeys though, we'd drop him off at Nain's. He'd have what he called his second breakfast, orange juice and a biscuit.

Anna looked at Nain. Remember? she said. Betty nodded.

The old lady spoke very quietly. I soon realised that, like Olwen, he had the gift. A special sensitivity. How would you describe it? A kind of second sight, maybe. Only neither of them saw the future. Just the past.

I didn't know anything about this at all at the time, said Mari, with what sounded like annoyance. Not then.

I didn't either, Mari, Anna said. There was no reason why we should. Though Bryn told me much later that he'd seen it for himself, very early on, after Kieran first arrived here. But he kept quiet about it. Didn't even talk to Kieran about it when he was trying to tell him he'd seen the old miners up on the tops. Bryn's way of handling it was to pretend it wasn't happening, in the hope that it would go away. He's changed in that respect recently. He does talk about it now. Doesn't he, Betty?

Betty nodded, and started to speak again. I noticed that by now Mari appeared to be sulking, but at last she was letting her grandmother tell her own tale. Bryn blamed me when Olwen upped sticks and ran off with Danny Walsh, you see, said Betty. According to him it was all because I'd filled her head with nonsense about the Guardian. According to him that was why she had to get away. But it wasn't as if I started it. It was already there. She had an instinct for it, a natural understanding. All I did was answer her questions as honestly as I could, though Olwen, and then Kieran after her, they both knew things that were beyond me. With Kieran, exactly because of what had happened with Olwen, I deliberately avoided mentioning anything about the Guardian. I'd taken on board what Bryn had said. Ted too, but he was nothing like as angry as Bryn was. Anyway, I had no intention of making the same mistakes again. But Kieran, in a roundabout way to begin with, as if he was testing me, well, he wanted an explanation for what his own experience was telling him. He wanted to know if I knew who the man was who he'd seen standing at the bottom of the hill that goes up to Hafod and Ffynnon Wna. He drew me a picture of him.

Betty held up the child's picture of the holly king, the one that was so crude and yet so powerful. This one, she said. Or one very like it. I'd never seen the holly king, of course, I didn't have the gift at all. But I knew the old stories. Celynnen was the place of holly, Maes Derwen the field of oak. I decided it would be wrong to fob Kieran off. I felt it was better to support him, guide him, if you like.

She was silent for a while and for the first time I noticed how loudly the old clock on the mantlepiece was ticking. In a way all that was happening now, going right back to the start – for me – when I found Kieran's things at the back of the wardrobe, was all about the strange freezing and thawing of time. I can't explain it in words. But I think we all felt it. And I felt sorry for my spiteful feelings towards Mari. I had a nerve to be getting at her. Sometimes things that are buried are best left that way.

Betty went on: I never saw things that were out of the ordinary, or felt things that were different from what other people felt. The tradition, for me, was a story, fascinating and special because it was part of our lives. Everything I knew I'd had to be told. Like my Taid before me, who'd been told in his turn by his grandmother. Now Olwen was a very different proposition. She had so much awareness. She sensed the presence of the past all around her. Not all the time. It would come and go. No warning, no accounting for it. Same with Kieran. Surely it would have been wrong to leave them floundering? I only told them the old stories about the Guardian and showed them the skull because they seemed to understand so much already. Though it was more like reminding them of something they'd known before, than telling them something new.

There was a lot of repetition and an almost sing-song quality to what Betty was saying now, as if she'd said this many times before. Taid and I, she continued, we had no idea what it was like to live with it: all that intensity. We had no idea what it meant to be open to all these echoes. But I don't think echo's the right word. It sounds too faded and far away. This wasn't. When I took Kieran to see the skull it was an interesting curiosity for me. That's all. Something I thought he ought to see. Part of his heritage. But for Kieran it was terrifying.

twelve

Bryn liked to keep his feet on the ground. That was his nature, and the ground he liked to keep his feet on was here, all around him. Reassuring, familiar. Its tawny shades, its frizzy textures. His cynefin. Just like his sheep. They were hardy Welsh Mountain Sheep. Generations of them, born and bred in and for this place. Hefted was the term for that. A good old-fashioned dialect word with a long tradition. He was hefted too. Just as the sheep were safe to wander on the common land of the mountain, sure of their terrain, a map of its winding paths encoded in their skulls, marked with their patches of favourite juicy grass, their places of shelter from storm, their choice shady spots in summer. Well, in terms of roots, and the way roots mean and matter, he was no different. The mountain, all its contours, all its hummocks and hollows, were in his blood and bones. But he would be the last of the hefted men of Celynnen, it seemed. Things were changing. There were fewer graziers on the mountain now, and it was no longer a livelihood to be passed on from father to son. He thought of his own sons, Huw and Sion. Huw still helped when he could, at lambing, at shearing time, whenever all the sheep had to be rounded up, for worming or whatever, but he had his own life to live. He'd made that very clear. He was buying his own place with his partner, Shelley, six months pregnant now with their first child, and he'd done well for himself, an electrician working for Airbus. Earned good money. Sion, though, was far afield. Second engineer on a gas ship, mostly in and around the Gulf. A life on the ocean wave, eh? Just about as far away as you could get from any notion of being hefted.

The mountain was full of memories for Bryn. He'd thought a lot about this lately, and he'd been thinking of Kieran too. It was a bit of a coincidence, strange really, that the girl should appear out of the blue just now. He'd felt something change in him in the last few months, in his attitude to his mother and her preoccupation with the traditions he'd always treated with such hostility. But it went back further, this change. It had been a slow process over a long period of time. He'd been feeling increasingly guilty, recognising belatedly just how cruel he'd been to Betty, and so unfair, blaming her for everything. For years now he'd tried to make amends but the guilt didn't go away. And now he saw things differently, as if all his sharp edges, the barriers he'd set up in childhood, had started to melt away. Perhaps the change in him began when Mari'd got interested in researching the history of the mountain, not just the factual, verifiable material, but the local tales, the legends. Folklore, if you like. And he saw, at last, that the factual history and this other, less tangible history were maybe not so foreign to each other after all.

Take Ffynnon Wna. A spring that welled up in a damp, darker green patch beneath one of the rocky outcrops on the tops, not unlike the much more dramatic Craig Rwlff. What was called the well consisted of a group of mossy stones, half sunk in the ground. It was widely documented that people had brought their horses up there for healing, and that those stones, now all higgledy piggledy, had once been shaped into a kind of circle, a large basin, or bath. Mari had heard it said that mares would be taken up there before being put to the stallion. So it was a fertility thing, too. He thought of the ponies Olwen had seen when, as far as he was concerned, there were no ponies there. And he thought of Kieran and his ghostly miners. He no longer felt that old surge. Of what? Anger? Jealousy? Fear? Or so he told himself. But just look at what had happened today. That old surge was exactly what he'd felt just now when Anna'd insisted the girl go with her to see Betty. He knew for sure now that it was a knee-jerk reaction. That even if in general his thinking had changed and mellowed, his behaviour somehow still seemed to follow its familiar reflex course, as if his body hadn't caught up with his altered attitudes. As if he'd been programmed to react in that way. Stop behaving like a bloody robot, he told himself.

Perhaps the land held its own memories, and some people could read them. There, was that such a revolutionary thing to say? Yes, he'd always maintained that it was. Had always refused, adamantly, to let such thoughts intrude into his sharply lit, clear-cut way of thinking. There was no room for shadows or vagueness, for shades of grey, not even for the truth of his own experience on that one, fleeting, blink-and-you'll-miss-it occasion, when what he'd seen didn't fit in with his scheme of things. Well, he was different now, and it was high time he was honest about it.

Some people had the notion that the brain was not so much a receiver as a filter. He could go along with that. Perhaps the filters just didn't work for the Olwens and Kierans. The land was encoded with messages from the past, that was it. And there were triggers that set some people off. Ok he had no idea how it worked and he didn't understand it but that didn't mean it didn't happen. For a while now, when he came up here to check on the sheep and blow away the cobwebs, he felt he was, how could he put it, at least less unsympathetic to the whole concept of land and memory, how they held each other together. So much so that Olwen and Kieran's mysterious and frankly worrying gifts no longer seemed so alien, so outlandish after all.

I may be going soft in the head, thought Bryn. But, d'you know something? I don't think I mind.

Then he remembered the last real conversation he'd had with Kieran. He'd banned him from going anywhere near Betty. This was after he'd been in hospital. They'd been so worried about him. God, it had been a nightmare. By all accounts the lad had screamed these blood-curdling screams when Betty'd taken him to see the skull, and then he'd fallen into a kind of fit. They'd got the doctor to him, and he'd been an emergency admission to hospital. He'd been catatonic. Well, slowly, he got better, but when he was finally fit enough to come home again, no way was Bryn going to risk letting Betty and her crazy Guardian stuff anywhere near him.

Or so he'd thought. But Kieran had stood up to him. You can't stop me going to see her, he'd said. She's always been good to me and she's the only person who understands.

Ahead of him, Meg scattered rabbits amongst the furze. He whistled after her and she turned to look at him, following reluctantly.

Bryn walked on, up to the highest point on the mountain. He could see Kieran so clearly, as if it were yesterday, a defiance he'd never shown before written in his stance and all over his face. Bryn could see the kitchen window behind him, the autumn wind billowing in washing on the line. What was he to do? He knew his intentions were for the best, but would it be wise to lay the law down now, with the lad in this vulnerable state? Even if it was for his own good?

Well, in the end Bryn didn't stop him going to see Betty, but from that day on barely a word was to pass between them. The atmosphere at Celynnen remained fraught and ugly, and within a fortnight Kieran was gone.

thirteen

It was a shaman's death, said Vanda. That's what Kieran's breakdown must've been. Different terminology, same thing.

When he saw the skull, said Jon, in a teacherish tone of voice, just for my benefit. The shock of whatever happened to him then, what made him psychotic, I suppose, brought about a change of consciousness. A kind of initiation.

Jon and Vanda are just about the most New Agey people you could imagine. Let's face it, I never even knew what New Age meant at all until I met Kieran. It was a kind of crash course, if you like. But there was always something very down to earth about him, unlike Jon and Vanda who are just so airy fairy. And sometimes very annoying. They were really getting to me right now, Vanda in particular. I'd given them a sort of edited highlights of what I'd found out at Celynnen, and now they were explaining everything back to me, as if I was stupid. I wanted to say to them, hey come on, I have read stuff about shamanism. When I was ill in Kieran's flat, apart from what he taught me, I had a good look at his books because I wanted to know where he was coming from, and I suppose, too, I was trying to impress him, letting him see I was taking an interest in what he was interested in. Bit pathetic that, maybe. Anyway, I know I've always put him on a pedestal.

By now Vanda was wondering whether the skull was actually so ancient it went right back to prehistoric times and was part of a human sacrifice. Perhaps Kieran with his special sensitivity had tapped into all that anguish and agony.

It would be interesting if we could get it carbon-dated, said Jon.

We? What were they thinking of now?

I've messed things up enough for these people as it is, I said. No way are you going barging in there...

Ok, said Jon. I'm not suggesting anything like that. I just thought it would be interesting, that's all.

Just then their meals arrived. As they tucked into their salad with melted brie wedges and redcurrant jelly, I thought about the things Mari had told me, sitting here an hour or so before. How when Kieran went missing, despite all the reassuring letters he left for everybody, Bryn had driven hundreds of miles looking for him, every spare moment he could find. Liverpool, first, the obvious place to start, then well into Lancashire, and to Manchester and beyond. Mari reckoned Bryn had had some kind of breakdown himself. Only he didn't break. He carried on, totally obsessed. He wasn't talking to Betty at all, and didn't for a couple of years, at least. And although she was in her first year at college, Mari was well aware that it was pretty hellish at home. It was round about this time that Sion ran away to sea, as she put it. And Anna started working part-time as a doctor's receptionist. They needed the money, yes, but it was just good to get out of the house. Bryn had become impossible. To make matters worse just before he left, Sion had turned on his father and accused him of caring more about Kieran than about him and Huw. He told him he couldn't understand why, either, since all Kieran had ever brought them was trouble. Quite unfair, that, she said. But perhaps understandable.

I didn't tell Jon and Vanda about any of this. It was none of their business. It was none of mine, either, of course, but I reckon Mari was never backward in coming forward. She was actually a much warmer and more straightforward person than she'd seemed at Celynnen and at Betty's. And there was obviously already a lot of tension between Anna and her. Families, eh? They're a minefield. I'd only had a quick snap-shot of it all but it seemed that everyone had their own take on Kieran's illness and his disappearance. And everyone had his or her own idea about the cause of it all and, of course, who was to blame.

But I'm getting the order of things all wrong. I ought to start with what happened back at Betty's cottage, just as she was starting to describe taking Kieran to see the Maes Derwen skull, and how he collapsed and was taken to hospital. Well, just then my mobile started to ring. Only it didn't just ring did it? It had to sing out at full volume with the silliest, stupidest ring tone in the world. I was so embarrassed I didn't know where to put myself. It was Vanda telling me they'd be later than they thought getting to The Black Lion where we'd arranged to meet and have a meal before going home. Even after I'd switched the thing off it seemed like the ridiculous sound of it was echoing on and on in all that silence and ten-sion, and then the baby started to cry. Things just went pear-shaped as if the scary point in Betty's story joined up with the baby's yelling and the farcical sound of my cartoon voices, everything exploding into chaos. It just went hysterical.

Mari started to see to the baby but Anna wouldn't let her. Leave things to me, she said, taking over with an in-your-face bossiness she hadn't shown before. She shook my hand repeatedly as she shepherded Mari and me out of the room, in a kind of panic, but formal somehow too, thanking me for finding them and telling them about Kieran and at the same time making it quite clear she wanted us out of there.

Perhaps Mari could take you to The Black Lion for a coffee, she said, then, at the door she mouthed her words in an exaggerated, almost pantomime way, I'm worried about Betty, she said. I think this has all been too much for her...

Perhaps Betty's reaction was exactly what Bryn had been afraid of, but there was so much more to it than that. A whole family saga of pain and recrimination. And me the messenger in the middle of it. Today was a day in which I was to see so many things from an entirely different angle, as if, beforehand, I'd always been in the dark, blissfully ignorant, if you like, (only less of the bliss, more of the just plain ignorant) and was now coming out into the light. Not that the light made things easier to take. Not a bit of it. Realising just how complicated people can be and how our own attitudes are often so simplistic, not so much plain wrong, though, as seeing only part of the equation. Being mentally lazy, in other words, and missing the whole point.

After Mari had gone, I'd sat there on my own in that dark-panelled lounge bar, thinking it all over. I felt so twitchy and restless. I'd really have liked to get out in the crisp cold and walk off all my disturbed feelings. But I had to stay put because I was waiting for Vanda and Jon to join me. When they finally arrived, I tried to tell them what I'd found out but this wasn't easy because Vanda kept interrupting, and half the time I couldn't get my head round it all anyway.

Mari'd suddenly realised something I think was very important as we sat there earlier. Why Kieran had changed his name from Walsh to Wood. He didn't feel any loyalty to Danny for a start. Why should he? He wanted to demonstrate to himself that he was going to start his life all over again. What better way than with a new name? But above all, his roots emerged from two farms with trees in their names. Celyn and Derwen. Holly and Oak. So Wood as his new name was an obvious choice, and showed that, at heart, he wasn't turning his back completely on everything that had gone before.

She went on as if she was talking to herself now. Maybe, by this time he already knew how, in the old religion, the holly king takes over from the oak king after the midsummer fires, she said. At the winter solstice it's the reverse. When Kieran came to Celynnen it was around midsummer. And he saw the holly king just at the time he comes into his own.

She looked at me now as if she'd suddenly remembered I was there. And she smiled as if she was trying really hard to lighten up.

Funny, isn't it, she said, to think of the waning year starting around midsummer? And the waxing year in the depths of winter?

I had an inspired moment just then. It's like the seed of the yin in the yang. And vice versa, I said.

Exactly, said Mari.

I hadn't liked her at all to begin with. Afterwards, without saying much more, really, I think we came to some kind of understanding. And I'm quite sure that up till that point she hadn't liked me either. So there you are.

After Vanda and Jon had finished their meal and it was time to think of getting off home, Vanda got up to go to the loo and Jon and I were just sitting there. I realised he was looking at me in a very hostile way. And Jon's the most mild-mannered sort of person. That's what I've always thought but, hell, what do I know?

Look, he said, and his voice sounded like it belonged to someone else. I know you think the sun shone out of Kieran's backside...

I couldn't believe this: the tone of his voice; the expression on his face. Though I realise now he must have had a real struggle trying to keep what he was about to say to me to himself for all this time. Obviously Vanda must have told him not to tell me. Which just goes to show how wrong I'd been about her.

Kieran was a great guy in many ways but he wasn't perfect, Jon went on. When you'd been sleeping rough and you were really ill, if it hadn't been for Vanda stepping in, it might have been a completely different story.

I just sat there staring at him.

He was giving you all these herbal things, he said, and to put it bluntly, you weren't getting better. Vanda said that if he didn't get a doctor to see you she'd get one herself. You actually had pneumonia and you were prescribed very strong antibiotics. The doctor wanted you to go into hospital. He wasn't exactly impressed by Kieran, or the set up in his flat, if you must know, so Vanda reassured him that she'd nurse you herself, and see you took the antibiotics.

I don't remember any of this, I said, feeling very small.

Guess why, said Jon. You were bloody ill, that's why. You could've died.

I didn't think he could get any angrier, but he could. You may not know it, but Vanda is a trained nurse. Sure, she's keen on complementary medicine, but she's got enough nous to know when conventional medical treatment's needed. Which is more than Kieran ever understood.

Before I had a chance to say anything else, he kind of muttered between his teeth, horribly, really. You ought to show Vanda more respect.

And then he stood up and disappeared off to the gents.

I was gobsmacked. When Vanda came back, looking even more immaculate than she had before, she sensed something was different. Jon and I weren't even so much as looking at each other so she said, nervously, is everything ok?

I looked at Jon but he obviously wasn't going to say a word, so I finally managed to blurt out something. Why didn't you ever tell me you nursed me when I was ill? My voice sounded guilty and thin. And about getting the doctor and everything?

What are we raking all this over for now? Vanda asked, looking at Jon very hard.

But he was paying for their meal at the bar and was out through the door before we'd even collected our things.

Kieran was a very special person, she said. Nothing changes that.

No, I said, then afterwards, thanks. She gave me the lightest touch on my arm.

Then I thought I'd ask her, on the off chance. Have you got any idea where Kieran went after disappearing from Celynnen, before turning up round our way?

There's quite a few missing years, she said. You know how secretive he could be.

I nodded. I'd always known there was stuff I didn't know about Kieran, but now I was just baffled. He'd let me think he'd cured me himself, hadn't he? That wasn't exactly authentic.

I know he did labouring work on building sites for a while, she said. Not sure where. And I know he was in some sort of, well, community. Somewhere high up in the Pennines.

D'you know anything about the girl in his paintings? I asked.

She died, Vanda said. That's all I know.

We were walking across the car park by now.

You know how he sometimes went to sweat lodge ceremonies, she said.

In Manchester?

Well, she smiled, Manchester's a kind of secretive shorthand for the general direction, I suppose, but it was on the side of a mountain, high up somewhere. And it was where this community was. Commune, whatever. He was still in touch with them.

She shrugged her shoulders. We none of us ever really knew much about him, did we? she said.

A silent Jon was sitting in the car looking straight ahead. And by the way he was tensing his shoulders he was still angry.

As we left Foel Gron behind us, I promised myself that I'd come back one day. When I'd got myself a decent job, had passed my driving test, all those things I planned to do. I wouldn't go near Celynnen itself. I wouldn't want them to think I was stalking them or anything, and let's face it, they'd already seen more than enough of me. What I wanted was just to see for myself, on my own, all the places Kieran had been happy in. I'd have a good look at that map again. There must be ways round to Craig Rwlff and Ffynnon Wna that don't involve going near the farm. Because so much of it's common land anyway, there's bound to be access.

fourteen

Hey, come on now, said Bryn as the sheep came butting and baaing, giving Meg a wide berth admittedly, but as ever hoping for extra helpings. He was pretending to shout at them now. I was up here first thing with bales for you. You greedy lot. You haven't finished all that yet.

The sheep knew the sound and the tone of his voice. Of course they did. But more than that; they recognised the familiar hum of the Land Rover's engine and its change of gear coming up the track long before the vehicle emerged into view. They'd be there, waiting. Ready and watchful. Ears erect, heads all pointed in one direction. Cupboard love, to be sure, but none the worse for that. Bryn got annoyed when people put sheep down as stupid. Not a bit of it. They could be shrewd in plenty. Opportunistic. Adaptable. And they had different personalities, just like people. They could be bold, even reckless. Neurotic, ingenious, timid and sly. You name it. A few were born leaders; most were happy to follow but there were others again who were just plain awkward. Stubborn. Rebels even. Together they possessed the collective intelligence of the flock, but within that flock there were individuals, as recognisable by their behaviour and the distinctive pitch of their bleating as by their marking, the thickness of their fleeces, the pattern of splodges on their faces.

Bryn walked on and upward, Meg at his feet one moment, then running off the next. She might be middle aged by now but she didn't know it, still as skittish and exuberant as a pup. He usually had two dogs, the one bringing up the other, but he hadn't had the heart to get another after Nancy had been run over last spring. Now Meg was young in spirit but she was actually quite sensible. A prudent dog. Poor young Nancy had been a wild child, had got out somehow and must have tried to herd a car somewhere on the way down to the village. Alun Nant Coch had found her, dreadfully wounded, literally trying to crawl back up the hill. Alun was no softie but he'd been visibly upset, and Bryn was just glad not to have seen that pitiful sight himself. They'd buried Nancy under the rowan in the front garden and afterwards Meg had followed him round, looking up at him, forlorn, as if asking, where's Nancy? Where's she gone?

There was so much more traffic on the mountain now they were trying to promote it as a leisure amenity. Ramblers and birdwatchers. Amateur botanists. Families on picnics. Speeding idiots too, of course. Bryn wasn't exactly overjoyed at the prospect of sharing his world with people who didn't appreciate its ways. To be candid he didn't really want to share it with those who did.

Meg came bounding up to him again. She was actually Meg Mark 2. Bryn felt as if he'd measured out his life in dogs. There'd been a Meg when he was a lad. She'd had a wonderful sense of humour. With his father she'd pretend to be disobedient, looking at him sideways on, to catch his exasperation. Seeing it, she'd then seem almost to laugh, you could see it, and dart up to him playfully for a pat, before carrying out the task she'd been bidden to do. In the end, man and dog played the game together. There'd never been a dog quite like the first Meg.

What were the names of the dogs twenty years ago, when Kieran arrived at Celynnen? He thought it was probably Benjy and Cariad. Yes, definitely Cariad. Dog and boy had thought the world of each other.

That first time up on the way up to the tops, when Kieran had caught that fleeting sight of the miners and Bryn had so briskly and forcibly whisked him away, he'd been about to show him the view over the estuary. They'd not got that far but on the next clear day they'd gone up there again, Bryn hoping desperately that Kieran wouldn't see anything out of the ordinary this time. It had taken him a while to figure out how quickly the boy learned to keep his strange sightings to himself. No wonder, after his illness, he'd insisted on continuing to go to Betty's house. Even if she had none of the gift herself she was able to give his sightings credence, and that must have reassured him. Bryn had come to see, too late, how pigheaded he'd been in trying to impose his ban, and how courageous the boy had been in standing up to him. Mari'd been right, not long after Kieran had gone, when she'd pointed out to him that what he'd needed most was consistency. He knew they all wanted the best for him but he'd come to recognise the way in which his presence created divisions in the family. That was the heartbreaking logic behind his disappearance. The ravening guilt that Bryn had experienced later, as he'd searched for him obsessively, but to no avail, then taking his failure out on Betty by blocking her out of his life, well, he could hardly believe he'd behaved like that now. The girl's arrival today had churned it all up. Even now, though, if he were honest, knowing what he knew then and feeling what he felt then, he was sure he'd behave in exactly the same way. Conviction's a terrible thing and he'd had buckets of it.

Mari did sometimes come out with things that made him think. Only the other day she'd been talking about memory, how it works. And sometimes how it doesn't. How memory can get it so desperately wrong because we see our own lives with only partial vision. We can get the substance but miss the essence. And the essence is what matters in the end. It's what, if we're lucky, we're left with after the filtration process of time.

What had Kieran remembered of Celynnen? Had his illness and those last jagged weeks spoiled all the happy times? How proud he and Anna had been of the way he'd thrived with them. He'd had bundles of nervous energy right from the start but he looked and surely was malnourished, spindly and undersized. How quickly he filled out and grew tall and strong, losing his city pallor, exuding a new confidence in everything he said and did. He shone with well-being. Up until that day when Betty had taken him to see the skull, his awareness of the past and its echoes didn't appear to trouble him. Assuming he 'saw things' fairly often, and Bryn still had no idea whether he did, his odd experiences dovetailed into the rest of his life with no apparent strain. And that, he'd come to realise over the years, was down to Betty.

Bryn stood looking down over the panorama before him, remembering that day long ago when the young Kieran had seen the view for the first time.

D'you know what that water is down there? Bryn asked him.

Kieran shook his head.

That's the River Dee, that is. The estuary where it runs out to the sea. And that land on the other side, d'you know what that is?

Is it England?

Well, yes, it's part of England. It's called the Wirral. Have you heard of that?

Again Kieran, so large-eyed and intense it hurt to see, solemnly shook his head.

Have you heard of Birkenhead?

Yes, said Kieran.

And what's the river there?

The Mersey, said Kieran.

And what's on the other side of the Mersey?

Liverpool.

Right, said Bryn. Some of those buildings we can see over there are in Liverpool. So where you come from isn't far away, is it?

I live here now though, said Kieran.

Lucy is Collecting Archetypes

She has quite a file already. Some are her own invention. Or maybe they are variations. Anyway, they're different, like The Old Woman of the Trees.

Here is her picture, in Lucy's drawing book that has a green cover like suede. Imitation suede, it's got to be. How can you have green suede? She remembers looking over the gate at calves in a field. Golden calves. She thinks of them as golden calves, but they were a gentle brown. Jerseys? Guernseys? She looked at the way their coats had patterns, whorls of growth, and she thought of suede. Then, suddenly, but of course that's what suede is made of. How horrible. She ought to be a vegetarian but isn't.

Here is The Old Woman of the Trees. She has drawn her in a grey cloak, billowing, with a hood so you can't see her face. This is because Lucy can't decide whether she's friendly.

Probably not.

Lucy has placed her in her special landscape. Each archetype has his or her own special landscape. This is Nevern in winter. Here is the cool triangle of Carn Ingli. Here is the church, the path, the bleeding yew. Here is the carved cross and here the holy stream.

But The Old Woman of the Trees is in the forest. As you'd expect. It's primeval forest. Lucy can see her now, the people she's leading, their speech all shorn to sibilants and gutturals. Here come the wild ponies, their hooves all pattering in a breath of frost. And the Old Woman herself, who speaks no words, telling it all through gesture and presence. You have to concentrate. Lucy does the movements in the lounge. It's the language of dance, a bit like tai ch'i but different. She knows the movements are right but only does them when no one else is there. Then Nurse Moira comes in with the drugs trolley and spoils it.

Ah, there you are Lucy, she says, and Lucy takes her tablets, appears to swallow them, but manages to anchor them in her teeth. She will slip out now onto the veranda, fish the tablets out, stick them in the soil around the bay tree in its tub. Across the lawn comes The Guizer, but look, there are two Guizers. Hare and Coyote. Hare stands on his hind legs and looks quite scary, taller than Coyote, who has a crumpled air this morning but still with that rich sheen in his grey coat.

Lucy is angry about something. She is thinking hard. Why won't the Hero come? He was there briefly in the dining room yesterday, but she could not catch his eye. Sometimes he is a young Egyptian king. A pharaoh. Sometimes he is a toreador. She passed him the roast potatoes in the white dish but he would not look at her. It was deliberate.

The Old Woman of the Trees has a gift for her, to compensate, maybe. She seems to be friendly after all.

Lucy holds out her hand, keeps the palm flat.

It is a butterfly made of ice.

Still glimpsing through the branches' thready selvedge, that clear-cut shape, that whitewashed gable end with its small square window. Turning deeper in where the path is softened, dampened, where the midges hang in their clouds, to shift as she skirts them, reassembling their tiny vivid life, collectively murmuring.

She had come back. They had welcomed her with tea on the low wall where she had found the yellow-banded snails

and where the washing hung like bunting. Their faces wore
the same serenity. Their voices made the same accepting
sounds. How could she tell them, here in this summer land
with the mare and foal, with the grey cat with the blue eyes,
what her life had been since, how a great wound had opened?
The language would be all wrong. It could not be spoken.

She must put down her cup. She must make some excuse.
She goes out through the side gate, staunchly smiling. There
might as well have been a flaming sword.

But Paradise takes many forms. Lucy sees The Old Woman
again, this time in snow. It is whiteout with happiness. She
feels the eagerness of a child but she is not a child. She is
staying with Rhodri in that funny little flat he's rented up at
The Firs. Once upon a time it was the granary and was joined
on to the farm. You have to be careful when you get out of
bed or you bang your head on the rafters. They look out on
snow, never so thick, so pure. She borrows an old pair of
Wellingtons. Even with three pairs of thick socks the boots
are miles too big, flop ridiculously on her feet, but who cares,
as they charge out into that pristine world, throw snowballs
at each other, slip and slide around and crunch in the deep
crispness. The air smells of cold and cleanliness, almost metallic. Where the lane joins the main road, where Himalayan
balsam grows in summer on the wide verge, there are bull-
finches like pink flares in the white, their colours a paintbox.
She licks her lips at the sheer gorgeousness of the contrast.
Their brilliance hurts her eyes.

She was in love with Rhodri. But Rhodri has gone. She
doesn't want to think about why he's gone. The Old Woman
takes over, takes her by the hand to the memory garden. Stone
doves. A praying child in marble. Hands together softly so.

Little eyes closed tight. She looks beyond the hood and sees The Old Woman's face for the first time.

What does she read in that face? Wisdom? Pain? She is her favourite archetype, this Old Woman of the Trees. She can trust her, can't she? Can't she? She gave her the butter-fly made of ice, didn't she? But the expression on the face wavers. Is ambiguous. Swimmy as water. No wonder she'd wanted always to hide it behind the hood. And then she's gone. The Old Woman's gone. The snow is gone. And Rhodri.

For good. Not nastily. Sadly. Which is maybe worse. And it all comes back. The reason. How he couldn't take any more. Any more. Of her. How erratic she was. That's what he said. How he just couldn't bear the way she'd become. So she's running in the corridor. But really there's nowhere to run. Which is why.

They've found out about her trick with the tablets. Or they've worked it out, most likely. She was always careful not to be seen. It isn't tablets any more, anyway. Now a nurse always stays with her while she takes her medication in syrup form in a little plastic cup. For a moment Lucy sees herself, tastes herself, as a white powdery tablet that's stuck in her back teeth, that bitter grittiness.

Dissolved now.

Your medication's prescribed to help you, Lucy, says Dr Fox. You do realise that don't you? He doesn't look like a fox. She tries to think of the Guizer in Coyote form. But can't bring him to mind. Can't make a picture in her eye. Nothing there but what's there. Chairs and a table. And curtains that are green with small white flowers. And a picture on the wall. A harbour with boats bobbing. The artist's got the reflection of the waves on the side of the boat. Shining. Which she thinks is quite cleverly done.

He wants to talk about when she was teaching. She doesn't. She doesn't want to think about it. She knows, for a start, that she doesn't even look old enough to be a teacher. The girls she was supposed to be teaching looked much older than her. Worldly wise. Streetwise. Why do they want to rub her nose in it all the time? It's like torture. They go on and on. They were her saviours, the archetypes. They are fading now. The Hero, when did she last see him?

The Old Woman stands at the edge of the trees. Look. She's going to turn her back on her. And Lucy knows that once she's gone back in where the trees grow so close together there's no light, well, Lucy knows she won't be coming out of there ever again.

Narcotic Crocus

It used to be a brothel, said Zoe.

You're joking.

Through an easy-to-miss door between a Thai restaurant and a newsagents and I'm following her up the stairs. A tiny landing at the top. A pathetic scrap of carpet looking as if it's sprouted there like some kind of mutant moss. Kitchen first. We dump all the shopping on the worktops, all the tons of food and half the booze for the party tonight. After the gig. It'll be some party too, a celebration and a goodbye. Zoe's had the nod that her PhD's been accepted. She's just got to spruce up some charts and photographs. Right now though she's more bothered about us all seeing the band tonight. Every night behind the Union bar for weeks now she's been telling us how brilliant they are. Her brother knows the bass guitarist and she's heard their demo CD.

Wait till you see this, she beckons.

When you hear there's a good place going you've got to move fast so I'd already agreed to take it on, sight unseen. This was my recce. Just that glimpse of the kitchen and it looked good, thin as a ship's galley but clean. A students' house and a clean kitchen! I'd struck gold. I can imagine Zoe's reaction if I'd said anything. Well, we are all post-graduates here, aren't we, she'd slur in a deliberately over-refined accent. But let's face it Zoe was posh to start with.

Great, I say. Her bedroom's a mess at the moment as she's been packing and there's clothes and things strewn every-where but it's a big room. High ceiling. These were once grand town houses after all.

Notice anything?

What d'you mean?

Observe the ceiling, Megan, she says. What do you see?

I don't know what I'm supposed to see. There are marks in the corners, all of them, as if something's been removed.

Mirrors, she says, giving me a sideways look.

You mean...

Yeah.

I thought it must've been long ago.

An historical brothel? No, child. Late eighties. Quite a high-class establishment, apparently. If you can't sleep you can always lie back and think about them. And their goings-on, she adds in a phoney Welsh accent just for me.

Even now I feel on show when I'm with Zoe. That I'm being tested. But I'm not uncomfortable the way I used be. I've really got to know her recently and I know she's had plenty of problems of her own.

Still. We go across to the big sitting room I'll be sharing with Jan and Alec. I've met them both and they seem ok. I'll get some peace here and that's the most important thing with my Finals on the horizon. It's a really stylish room, big sofas covered with cream-coloured throws, lots of plants every-where. We're near Featherstone Corner here, on one of the main roads into the town centre, and looking out we seem surprisingly high up. The double glazing's effective. There's just the faintest swish of sound from the traffic. Then I realise it's snowing. Just the odd flake for starters. But soon it's swirling fast and all the cars have their lights on. Some of them coming in from the direction of the motorway have small pillows of snow on their roofs and bonnets, and the sky's a pregnant grey.

It's not going to stick, says Zoe.

So you're a meteorologist as well as a molecular biologist?

Intuition, she says. I thought you literary types were into all that.

I couldn't stay long. Mr de Silva wanted me at the shop by three so it's just a quick cup of coffee as we stand there in the window watching the snow. Like big kids. What happened next I didn't pay that much attention to, not then. I heard a child crying.

Is there a flat above this one?

No. Just empty attics.

Can't you hear it?

What?

Listen. There's a kid sobbing its heart out.

What are you on? she says.

I'm not in Zoe's league. Now that doesn't mean I'm ashamed of my working-class background. Or that I put her on a pedestal. Nothing like that. My getting to university was the most upwardly mobile thing to happen in our family since the day we bought our council house, yes, but I wasn't going to let myself be dazzled by anyone's social clout, or money, or savoir faire. Or brains. Or looks. I'm getting defensive, aren't I? Our paths would never have crossed at all if she hadn't turned up at the Union bar early last term. Post-grads and undergrads don't mix much, let's face it. Especially when it's Science v Arts. I'd been working there since my third week as a fresher. Glass collecting to start with. I needed every penny I could get. And it was when I was looking for cheap set texts in Mr de Silva's second-hand bookshop that I cheekily asked if he needed someone part-time.

You have an honest face, he said. Which was nice.

So I work all day Wednesday at Browsers, and once in a while for an odd hour or two, like today, when he's got something on. And in the Union bar most nights. I'm trying to keep my debt just about manageable.

Right, I admit it. I was bloody annoyed when Zoe got to start pulling pints straightaway, especially when it was often me who had to tell her which glasses to use. She was quick though, mixing cocktails with unnecessary flamboyance before you could say Tequila Sunrise. How come? Well, our clientele went upmarket immediately in her wake, which I reckoned was the reason why Vincent had taken her on in the first place. Someone said they'd been an item way back. In his dreams. But what puzzled me was why she'd wanted the job in the first place. She couldn't have wanted the money. Not with her background Her father's some bigwig academic at LSE and her mother's the biographer Phoebe Hilliard. Even I'd heard of her. And everything about Zoe spoke money, her clothes, her classic Mini Cooper, her expertly layered hair. But I got to learn so many unexpected things about her I had to scrap all my assumptions. My prejudices too. It works both ways. Come to think of it, getting to know Zoe was an education in itself.

I've got to get to Browsers. I mean fast. Telling Zoe I'll see her tonight I clatter down the stairs and out onto the slippery pavement. There's usually a bus from here to Presbyter Street every ten minutes but today the weather's messed up the timetable. I'm just about to give up and start walking when one appears. I'm going to be late now, anyway. Hell, I hate that. And it's still snowing, sticking too. Despite Zoe's forecast. Hardly at all on the street but a lot where it gets some peace, on shop awnings, roofs and chimneys, and the equestrian statue in Wellington Square.

The next stop after I get on, this little old lady sits in front of me. She's all shades of beige and cream and fawn with dangly earrings that don't match. She turns round and pounces.

I've ended up with a head of white hair, she says, whipping off her little crocheted hat. Now I can do without garrulous old biddies. My lovely old Nan's got Alzheimer's and it's a sore point. I try to smile non-committedly.

Yes, she says. All this white hair. Just look at it.

I do. It's snowy and thick. She shakes her head as if she's in some ad for senior citizens' shampoo.

You've got lovely hair, I tell her.

Thank you. Her eyes glitter. And do you know, I've got a white cat. And he sits on the back of my chair and he goes woosh with his paw like this. He thinks I'm a cat.

I dig in my bag and pull out *The Collected Plays of Christopher Marlowe.*

Now she's turned to a skinny lad on our right. Across the aisle. The hat's back on and we get an action replay.

I've ended up with this head of white hair. And I've got a white cat. He goes woosh with his paw...

She gets no encouragement from grey Nikes, so she selects another victim, an intensely respectable uptight old bloke in the seat in front of her. Tweed coat with the collar up. Bottle-brush moustache. All human life is here. She actually leans over and taps him on the shoulder. You could do an interesting sociological study of good ol' British reticence on this bus.

I've ended up with this head of white hair...

Oh Gaawd. We get it all the way to Presbyter Street where I get off.

The refrain of it's in my head. Mr de Silva's in the shop

door looking peeved. Sorry I'm late, I say. To deflect his annoyance him I give him White Hair and Fawn Hat. I put on a show. Who needs Street Theatre?

Mrs Dauncey, he says. Wife of the late Professor Dauncey, a brilliant clarinettist in her day.

I can't put a foot right, can I? I wish I'd said nothing at all. Mr de Silva looks different. He's unusually smart in a dark suit. Is there a lady in his life? Is it a meeting with the bank manager? I'll be back by five, he says.

Ok.

It's very quiet. I've been sat here an hour getting well stuck in to Dr Faustus when the door opens and three unusual (to put it mildly) customers come in. Two bleach-blonde girls, sisters I suppose, thirteen, fifteen, thereabouts and an older woman. Their mother. Haggard. Hardly any teeth. The younger girl's wearing a very short denim skirt, artistically frayed at the hem. I notice because her legs are blue with cold. Literally.

Is the man in? says Haggard. We bought these books off him and he said he'd give us our money back if we didn't like them.

Really?

Yeah. You calling us liars?

No. Not at all. It's just not Mr de Silva's usual policy.

Look, says big sis. We don't care what his poxy policy is. We just want our money back. Right?

I'm afraid you'll have to see Mr de Silva. He's back at five.

I've sussed it. They've stolen these books. Must've. The main stand in the front's just paperback fiction and they could easily have nicked them if Mr de Silva was in the back.

It's Haggard's turn again. Now listen to me, dear, she says, her voice gone sickly syrupy. We don't want any trouble do we?

Are you threatening me? I say, to my surprise. I suddenly realise I'm almost enjoying myself. They'd obviously expected me to be nicey-pie.

Big sis has gone red in the face. We could sort you any day, she says, but she's more pathetic than scary.

Any more of this and I'm calling the police.

Haggard again. We only want what we're entitled to, dear. Whining now.

Don't we all, I think. And then frayed denim grabs the books herself. It's like she's embarrassed and it's coming off her in waves. Come on, Mum, she says. You won't get owt off this posh bitch.

Me? Posh bitch?

Now the books come slither and thump on the counter: two Mills and Boons, a Danielle Steel and a Catherine Cookson.

Big sis glowers at me. You can keep your sodding books, she says.

It's one of those days alright. I sell some physics text books, Guy de Maupassant's short stories (in French) and a biography of Charles de Gaulle. I've just sold a book on the geology of the Aran Islands and I'm writing the title down when Mr de Silva appears. It's ten to five.

I want you to be the first to know, Megan, he says. I've put the shop up for sale. Going to concentrate on the antiquarian side now. On the internet. I'm getting too long in the tooth for this lark.

I gulp. Well that's my job gone. He reads my mind. I can't envisage a quick sale, so your job's safe for a while yet. No need for you to worry. And by the end of June it'll be fresh fields and pastures new, for you, anyway, won't it?

There's a sadness in his voice that's touching. I'd never

thought of Mr de Silva as old. Really old. But all of a sudden he looks it. I was going to tell him about Haggard and Daughters but just can't somehow. As I'm leaving my mobile rings. It's Vincent. Apparently Narcotic Crocus are stuck in the snow somewhere. What? Their van broke down. Narcotic Crocus? Oh, of course, Zoe's art-school wonder band. I'd forgotten all about them. This means it'll be busy in the Union bar after all. When there's a gig everyone drinks in the Syndrome and that's why he'd allowed me the night off. Now he wants me back. I tell him I'm supposed to be going to Zoe's party, knowing even as I'm saying it that I'm not being assertive enough. Still, I've got to keep well in, haven't I? I want to keep my job and there'd always be plenty of takers for it.

Yeah. She told me about that. If you just work till ten, that'll do, he says.

Bloody Zoe, I think. And guess who must've given Vincent my mobile number in the first place.

Now this is the bit that gets difficult. Writing about it, I mean. This is when the figures go off the graph and I don't want to write it down at all. It's like making it real. And for me it'll never be real.

Cursing Zoe and wondering whether I could be bothered to go to her pesky party at all, I went down the cellar steps to get a crate of mixers. She was there. Bloody hell, just for a moment. Zoe in the flesh, sat on the floor by the big defunct dishwasher, crying, mascara running down her face, hugging her knees and rocking back and forth. This was a re-run of what happened that night back in November when she opened up to me and told me about, well, her life. How she'd always been the odd one out at home. The scapegoat. Two brothers and a sister loved and wanted, her just used and abused. She'd got herself in such a state she was retching silently. I held her as she writhed. Told me about her bulimia. Told me how she was locked in her bedroom weekends and holidays. It was at this point I began to get suspicious. Just a bit. I couldn't imagine the Zoe I knew taking all this. But there again, perhaps, if she'd been just a little kid then? Anyway, I usually give people the benefit of the doubt until I'm proved wrong. It went on and on. How she only had a tiny college grant for her research and some money from the Thurling Foundation. How her parents were refusing to help her financially. How she'd had to go on the game to make some money once the bank had got distinctly shitty, as she put it. Was all this true? Any of it? I didn't know. But the agony felt real.

And then I blinked and she was gone.

There was no one there. I was seeing things, losing it big time. And then I was hearing things. The crying kid I'd heard before in Zoe's flat. That child sobbing.

I went up the steps with the mixers.

What's the matter with you? said Vincent.

I'm ok I said. I could hardly tell him, could I?

It was actually dead in the bar that night, what with the snow and the let-down with the band. I'd have liked it busy, to take my mind off what had happened. I wasn't under that much stress surely? To be seeing things like this? Hearing things? I went looking round for stuff to do just to try to get rid of the images, the sounds. Like taking the big grill apart that's never used anyway and scrubbing it, then mopping the cellar steps, putting up that yellow safety notice with the picture of the little matchstick man falling down. I felt a bit hysterical really but hiding it well. Trying to. Even if Vincent thought I'd lost the plot alright he didn't know why. Then at a quarter to ten, just when I was thinking I'd become quite a connoisseur of clock-watching, I was surprised to see Jan and Alec come in, their faces telling me something was wrong as soon as I saw them in the door.

They'd just come from the hospital. The party hadn't really got going when Zoe collapsed and went into convulsions. An ambulance and a team of paramedics got there very quickly working on her for what seemed ages. It was no good. Dead on arrival at St Mark's. The cause of death was revealed as a cerebral haemorrhage. The inquest revealed more. That Zoe had a serious cocaine habit. It turned out that Jan and Alec knew she was a user, but not the extent, and greenie little me had known nothing at all. They told me that she'd become addicted to online gambling too. That her parents had always supported her generously till her debts had just gone through the roof.

So how and where does all that leave my feelings about you, Zoe? I'd just handed in an essay for American Lit: assess the reliability of the narrators in *The Turn of the Screw* and *The Great Gatsby*. Kind of appropriate, huh? Wherever you are, with your posthumous doctorate and your fantasies, I'll never be able to get my head round you. Who were you, really? That apparition in the cellar, was that when you actually died? Why did you come to me? And that crying kid in the attic. Can you experience a ghost in advance of the facts? But a younger version? I don't want to think about it.

If anyone had asked me I'd have said I didn't believe in ghosts at all but, hell, it seemed I'd already met yours twice. I didn't move into your flat.

Birth of an Oxbow

*Under the ice there is movement. Under the ice which
has frozen then thawed then frozen again till it's layered
like flaky pastry, layered thin as if the ice was breathing
and its breath was caught.*

Immediately Judith wants to pick up a red marking pen
and correct it... layered thin as if the ice *were* breathing
and its breath *were* caught. She smiles at her own tiresome
predictable reaction. After all this time.
  But further back in time again when she was a different
person. A child...
  So cold the air creaks. Two of them, and a dog.

*And now the river is one clenched glittering waste across
ice meadows, the broad meander lost under a white crust.
They have seen nothing like these great fields of ice, ever.
Only the row of willow pollards, stumped spiky fists, can
tell you where the river is.*
  *And when the thaw comes it is sudden. Overnight the
ice is warmed as if someone took a blowtorch to it. And
the ice is no longer ice. It melts with a noise like a detona-
tion, but that's only the first. Now there's a sequence of
small explosions. The ice moves as it melts. It breaks the
banks, churns them away, leaving the willow pollards
stranded. And that old river bend is history, a cut-off
crescent. A remnant lake they call an oxbow.*

And Jinny, too, is history.

But history is more alive for Judith now than what's happening at this moment. And the dead are more present, more real to her than the living. Since Bob died she has entered a limbo. At first it was a strange cold place, an empty terror but it has become home for her, this limbo. And as she moves round this suddenly-so-much-larger house (is it the house that has become larger or is it herself that's somehow shrunk?) she meets Bob's presence. It's finer, this presence, totally non-physical and consequently the essential Bob, his thoughts, his feelings. None of the bluster. None of those qualities of the benign bully that had made him such a good teacher. This was a more tentative, more poignant Bob than she had ever known.

She'd told herself, at the beginning, that all this was decidedly unhealthy. And so unlike her. She should get out more, make an effort to meet people, take up some of those invitations she'd had from long-standing and well-meaning friends. And some of them lived in the most appealing places. Like Meryl and Jim in Keswick, for instance. Wouldn't it be delightful to be in the Lake District right now? Who was she trying to kid? She was happy where she was. Though happy was hardly the right word. Among familiar surroundings, anyway, familiar things that were Bob's as well as hers. This was Bob's bed, as much as it was her bed, and always would be. His clothes still hung in this wardrobe. His books were still on these shelves. If she went away, even for a day or two, that presence that still breathed here, that still existed in this subtle minor key, well, it might pine for her in her absence, up sticks and go. And she didn't want it to go.

She felt, and maybe it was crazy but she still felt it, that this

Bob that was dead needed her around more than the brash confident live Bob had ever done.

But it wasn't just Bob who was with her still, in the limbo place they seemed both to inhabit now. There were other people too. Memory people, going back to the time before she'd even met Bob. Vivid presences, long since gone, but suddenly revitalised. Judith flicked through the yellowing pages in the old box file. She'd forgotten all this stuff, written in her post-grad, teacher-training year. They'd been told to revisit their childhood, think themselves back to how a child feels and thinks and perceives, re-enter places they'd known as children, relive those experiences. Capture them again. It had been the late sixties when she'd written this, and she'd kept it, returning to it once or twice over the years because its freshness was convincing, was real somehow. Only now, in limbo land, floating as she was in a place that was so much more composed of the past than the present, it was as if she'd entered a flashback that was more than filmic. Perception. Sensation. She could breathe ice air. She could touch the rough textured wood of the hand rail on the stairs to the granary. It all combined. Grew. Spread.

Yesterday, reluctantly, she'd had to face up to the fact that Gareth and Co (that's what Bob had called them) would be here soon for Christmas. There was no escaping that. So it was about time she cleaned the large spare room where Gareth and Shani would be sleeping, and the room over the landing where the girls would sleep. She went in to that room first. It smelt faintly musty so she opened the window. With difficulty. They'd replaced the windows at the front of the house some years ago but these were the original old sash windows. She had to push and tug. Then she'd got up on a chair and started to sift through all the boxes and folders on top of the wardrobe. She hadn't sorted through these for years. And that's where she'd found *The Birth of an Oxbow*.

In the kitchen Judith's mother sits darning socks. The shiny wood mushroom glints through the hole in the thick grey wool. The large-eyed needle draws its soft grey trail. Background is a warm bubbled scent of chicken bones for stock steaming gently on a low heat.

It was like this the winter before you were born, says Judith's mother. Children from the top farms didn't get to school for nine whole weeks.

Judith draws snowflakes for Miss Harrison. Patterns of snowflakes. Each one different.

Memory swivels on scents. Not the scents of this drowsy kitchen, her mother's kitchen. No, these memory scents are fierce and primitive. Atavistic scents.

They belong to Tyddyn Hir, where Jinny lives. To Ty Pella over the yard, to Nain Lodwick's cottage. The tilting floor of dark slate flags. The dresser and its blue crocks. Cats' pee. Boiled cabbage. Musty flesh. And maybe more than a hint of old lady's pee.

Outside and scents is too fine a word. Smells. Stinks. Stenches. The gutter from the shippon. The dung heap fermenting its circlet of pissy puddles, its strong brown rivulets.

Come on. Climb the stone steps, there, sideways to the barn. Past the postbox in the wall, the stand for the churns, deep in the lane where the ivy flowers in November, bringing great daft flies, blue gold, buzzing feebly in fallen pollen. Up those stone steps to the granary loft as the door creaks open.

Another smell, a good one this. Wholesome and glowing. Grainy. A floor of teeming chicks. Sharp yellow mostly but also the softest beige and lemony. Cheeping round the incubator. Such a huge and tiny constant din. And the ropes of cobwebs on the beams splendid with dust and gold spiders. Move gently. Watch where you put your feet. The floor is simmering small chirpings. Judith picks up a chick. So fragile, so warm and alive. Trembly. It shits softly in her hand. It pecks at her fingers.

Jinny is dead. Nain Lodwick is dead. Uncle George and Puddles and all the cats, scrawny tortoiseshell around her door. Eyes blue as speedwell, there they play, scrambling, tumbling, in and out of the fancy wrought-iron legs of the mangle.

And the fizzy little bantam cocks are dead. And the purple mallow flowers growing like a huge bouquet out of the old stone pigsty without a roof. And the farm itself is dead. And buried. Lost under garages and gardens. Sheds and children's slides. Barbecue pits and carports, rotary washing lines.

Boxing Day. They have survived Christmas anyway. The first Christmas without Bob. Gareth and Shani have gone through with the ritual visit. Judith imagines their conversation. Shani would have much preferred an extended skiing holiday and Gareth is telling her how they really must go to Judith's. There'll be no getting out of it. She'll be on her own and no one should be alone for Christmas. Why ever not? thinks Judith. And though the words play only in her head they seem to have acquired a satirical tone that is more Bob's than her own. As for the girls, Haf and Lleucu would prefer to be elsewhere. Of course. Twelve and nearly fourteen now, inhabiting that exclusive teenage planet parents and widowed grandmothers enter at their peril. It was different when they were small but they're far too cool and sophisticated for all that Christmas stuff now.

And then Judith thinks of the oxbow. Why not? She has a sense of perverse mischief. What a good idea for their Boxing Day walk! She thinks of Bob, the novice geography teacher, the first time he saw the just slightly oozy summertime crescent, its new willows, mere saplings, the leaves yellow-green blades with darker nodules on the underside. What were they? Some sort of blight? Some kind of gall? It's as if she can hear birds in the branches, smell the riverside smell, feel, for a moment, summer sun on bare legs, bare shoulders.

That was a living geography lesson you know, he'd said. Amazing. You were really privileged to see that happening.

Nothing satirical there. The real thing.

Tyddyn Hir was already abandoned, awaiting demolition. She told him about Jinny. How at the start of her mother's long illness, Jinny had come to help. Supervised her bath night. Washed her hair. It was like being massaged by a tank. There was nothing delicate about Jinny and she soon learned to wash her own hair thank you, to escape those heavy, hearty hands bashing her up against the sides of the wash basin and the taps.

In the kitchen she'd shown her how to make pippin a scribbin. Hot milk and grated spice. And they'd play rowdy games of Strip Jack Naked with a pack of greasy cards. What a tactile, textured childhood she'd had. So rooted in time and place. Not like now. She looks at the two fashion-conscious little madams walking ahead on the sandy path high above the river. In sheltered places near the blackthorn hedge the grass is still white with frost, the oxbow, that long-lost meander to the right of them over the fields, the willows tall now, the alders' branches purplish against crisp December light. They're oblivious to their surroundings, these little townies. Lleucu spends all her time texting her friends in Penarth. Haf just looks bored. ok thinks Judith. You won't be coming here again. You won't be coming to our house again. I'm selling up. I'll buy an apartment in one of those new blocks by the sea. One bedroom only. That's all I need. And Gareth and Shani, you too. No more duty visits. They won't be necessary. Media babes, the pair of you. More at home in virtual reality than the real thing. We don't have to pretend anymore. You're free. I'm free. Let's be honest shall we?

She thinks of Bob. She thinks of Jinny. And she has a momentary sense of something akin to horror. That somehow, even dead, Bob and Jinny are still more robust, more real than these young, attractive fashionable people. Her flesh and blood maybe but somehow fleshless, bloodless. Alien.

Omigod, Bob had said, years ago when the two young marrieds had first come to stay. I never thought I'd have to use the word uxorious but that's what my son is.

Bob had disliked Shani intensely. Judith, the peacemaker, had always done her best to make her feel at home. Waste of time. She was so full of condescension, so effusive. And always acting. She couldn't be real if she tried.

She looks at her now. Shani smiles, but it's a slightly tentative smile. How unusual. Could it possibly be that she senses something's wrong? Is she actually that sensitive?

Judith's feeling something quite new to her. The liberating pleasure of long-repressed spite. She's almost giddy with a sense of liberation, underscored by her deep, never-quite-to-be-healed wound. And she knows when she gets back to the house there'll be less of Bob there. Knows for sure that he'll fade and fade. But it doesn't matter. He doesn't belong to externals. He's not outside her at all. He's in her. In her bones. Part of her.

Have we got enough now? asks Judith. Jinny straightens, braces a hand against her back. But memory selects and edits, makes her brisk and strong. Etches her forever against ice and dark trees.

Plenty. Can you manage that branch? You'll have to drag it yourself all the way. Judith nods. I can do it. Uncle George can saw it up for logs, can't he? Jinny stoops again. This time she sorts out the sticks. Makes a manageable bundle of them, hitching it under her arm. Her coat, bottle green, is threadbare round the pockets, the buttons, the cuffs.

Three shapes that could be medieval. Picking kindling along the high-water line. A woman, a girl. And a dog.

Puddles has scuttled off in crisp, powdered snow. Sniffing. Snuffling. A mystery. Everything smells of cold nothing. There's a wall-eyed collie in that dog. That and a lot more. Ugly really. Walking stiffly in the lane on his ancient bones. Panting. His lolled tongue steaming against the cold. They are both old, Jinny and Puddles. Memory glides and pounces. Evades. Enhances. Swoops in on detail. The icy air makes your chest hurt.

But if you smash down on the thick-iced puddle with the hard sole of your Welly, the ice crust shatters. Mosaic splinters. Like a mirror cracking. And if you move the hard sole of your Welly sideways like this, forcing down here, lifting there, look, liquid tadpoles. Little pockets of water, squeezing out under the ice. Creeping out. Like long commas. Or tears.

The thaw is coming.

Thin white hair peeks out from under Jinny's head-scarf, the silky blue one with the ducks on it. It is drawn taut, knotted under her chin. The winter glare catches her glasses. Makes them flare. The low sun on the water meadow makes them goggles of flame.

The Trip

Say what you like about Americans, they know how to make you feel at home. Just minutes after I'd clambered off the Greyhound, people I'd never met before were greeting me like a long-lost nephew. Helen and Dougie Edwards were determined to give me a welcome I'd never forget. Years ago Helen had been in the same class as my mother at school, and Christmas and birthdays ever since they'd kept in touch.

D'you feel like you're really Americans by now, I asked them. They looked at each other. Sure, we're Americans, said Helen. We've been here twenty-three years.

But we're Welsh Americans, Dougie said. Don't you forget it.

When we got to their house, very stylish and split level, a bit Frank Lloyd Wright even, there were four letters for me. My parents knew I'd be getting to Denver at some point in my backpacking adventure of a lifetime, so they'd written to me at Helen and Dougie's. It was the fourth letter, bulkier than the others, that stopped me in my tracks. It was full of wedding photographs. For all sorts of reasons I wasn't sure I could believe my eyes.

I suppose it all really begins one night at the end of August two summers back. I'd been waiting on at Puccini's, playing my usual game of pretending to be Italian. It made the work less boring and I reckon it got me better tips. Anyway, it had just gone midnight, and as I came out of the air-conditioned restaurant I was hit by the wall of heat outside. I imagined what my room at Dylan's would be like and I couldn't face that particular oven. Not just yet. Paint has stuck the windows together so you can't open them. So, although I was pretty well knackered I walked down to the harbour – even if the tide was out there'd still be cool air from where the river runs in.

Then through the darkness from the direction of the Blue Bridge came the grumbling whirr of the police helicopter. From where I was I couldn't actually see its livery, but there's nothing else that comes flying over the West End in the middle of the night. I thought it was a bit early for trouble, mind, since chucking-out time at some of the clubs wasn't till two, which is usually when the fun begins, and it doesn't usually deserve the helicopter.

Further down the seafront people were rushing out of the nightspots to see what was going on. I reckoned that by the time I got down there it would be all over anyway, so I didn't rush, but curiosity got me in the end and I followed the crowd. They were buzzing. The helicopter was hovering over the Hyper. By now it was shining its search beams up and down that warren of streets. There were loads of people out-side the club and more coming out all the time. It was panic, girls crying and hysterical, guys looking just plain numb. Two police cars and two ambulances rolled up, sirens blaring, followed by a third police car just a few minutes later. Now this just had to be the most exciting thing that had happened here for ages. Whatever it was.

It was actually very bad. Someone had been pushing a load of decidedly dodgy E, if it was E at all. Toxicology reports at the inquest said it had been a potentially lethal cocktail of mood-enhancing drugs. Well, it was more than potentially lethal, wasn't it? Seven people had collapsed. One of these died that night. Four more were in intensive care.

And one of these was Tanya. Strange that because she doesn't go to the Hyper usually, and as far as I know she doesn't take anything either. It was the hen night of one of the girls she works with.

I couldn't believe that Dylan could get himself a girl like Tanya. She could've had just about anyone. Hey, she could've had me! And she chose him. All of which goes to show how deeply weird women are.

Just to put you in the picture about Dylan. He's my cousin and he's two years older than me. Not that I've ever looked up to him. Ever since we were little kids I've always thought he was a complete wally. And when he was supposed to have grown up he wasn't any better. He did get to college but it lasted just three weeks. Then his dad took him into his building firm and that didn't last much longer. In the end a caretaking job was invented just for him. My Uncle Elwyn bought this rundown flat-let house in Gardenia Street, did it up, and gave Dylan the job of keeping an eye on things, hoovering the landings and being in charge of the Toilet Duck. Even he could manage that.

Dylan's got his own flat there of course and that's where I was staying, saving on bus fares home while I was earning all the money I could lay my hands on for this trip to the US. I'd got myself two jobs, working at Puccini's in the evenings and The Black Cat in the day. I like the atmosphere in the arcades: no, really. Perhaps I'm just a big kid but I like those flashing lights and that crazy noise. I'm in the change booth some of the time and if there's any problem with the machines I get on to maintenance, but generally I'm just walking round with a big bunch of keys on my belt, looking tough. It's acting, which I like to do, like being the Italian waiter. Practice for when I'm a legal eagle. I reckon there's a lot of acting in that.

I haven't said anything about Dylan's other incarnation. Friday, Saturday and Sunday nights he's resident DJ at Le Nautique Lounge, a place that's not exactly the epitome of cool. Reckoning that his real name, Dylan Warburton, is a bit too much for showbiz circles he calls himself Dillon Burton, specialising in Sixties and Seventies nights in his very own Golden Oldie Land. God, it's embarrassing.

We were all shaken up about Tanya. She seemed to pull through ok though, and after ten days she was home at her parents', convalescing. And then came the big shock. She had a stroke, a serious one, paralysed all down one side. She couldn't walk or talk. I went to see her just the once. I couldn't bear to see her like that. You've got to hand it to Dylan though, his whole life still revolved around her. He wanted them to get married, like they'd always planned to do, but she said she'd only marry him if she could stand beside him at the altar and say her words so everyone could hear. Fat chance of that, I thought. That's just wishful thinking...

Since Tanya's stroke and my inability, I suppose, to handle it, I'd given Dylan a wide berth. I was back at college, anyway. No messing about now. I was working really hard for my finals. It was tough but I knew I was luckier than most, knowing I was already fixed up. I'd be taking my articles at Hughes and Hayden-Ward; they're the best law firm around, easy. And as soon as I finished my finals I'd be off to the States. I just couldn't wait to go.

But I haven't told the whole truth about Tanya. How I pestered her. How I wouldn't take no for an answer, refusing to believe she could possibly prefer Dylan to me.

The very first time I saw her, it's still so clear, she was sitting at the little breakfast bar in Dylan's kitchen, perching

on one of his naff bar stools. She had long, long legs, lovely
slim brown legs. She had long hair to match and a face that
wasn't conventionally pretty, more interesting than pretty,
maybe. It was a strong face, big mouth and big nose. Hey,
I'm not describing her at all well. This way she sounds almost
ugly. What came over was her energy, her friendliness. And
then I saw her green eyes. It was her eyes and her smile that
made her beautiful, because, no doubt about it, she was
beautiful. Now I don't usually notice the clothes girls wear,
being more interested in what's underneath, in a laddish sort
of way, but I noticed what she was wearing that first time I
saw her. It was a short, kind of figure-hugging dress, dark
green crushed velvet. She was magnificent.

And this was Dylan's girlfriend?

I moved in fast, made it quite clear I was interested. She
wasn't. Not a bit. And I made the bad mistake of putting
Dylan down – that made her look at me with, there's only one
word for it, contempt. I was a real pillock. Even then I would-
n't leave her be, convinced she'd succumb to my superior
charms eventually.

She didn't.

What a lovely girl, said Helen when she saw the photographs.
She looked at my mother's letter, reading out loud how
Tanya's father had wheeled her down the aisle; and how very
slowly, levering herself up on the arms of her wheelchair,
she'd managed to stand by herself.

Isn't she beautiful? And so brave, said Helen. It's Elwyn's
son she's married, Dougie. He's just a bit older than you, isn't
he Jonathan, if I remember right. He looks a real nice guy.

Yes, I said.

It was summer and it was dusty and hot, but before I actually got there I always thought of Denver as a winter place: snow, skiing, pine forests. That night I dreamt of the Denver I'd had in mind.

I was all kitted up for winter sports, nothing but the best, very conscious of how I looked, the winter sun glinting on my shades. I was standing at the bottom of a ski lift, looking up as the cars climbed to the summit. Above me, the cars moved slowly and I was able to focus on the faces of the people. One couple in particular caught my eye, it was Dylan and Tanya. Like a big kid I waved and waved at them excitedly, and then strangely I saw that they were in the next car, and the next. The whole, slowly moving sequence of the ski lift now carried no one else, just identical versions of Dylan and Tanya, only by now it wasn't so much a ski lift as a huge shiny Ferris wheel like the one at Golden Bay back home. Still moving very slowly though, sort of solemn. No excited squealing or anything.

Somehow, and I can't explain it, I was scared. I felt I had to reach out to them, make contact with them, that it was incredibly important. I had to let them know I was there. I kept on waving, even though I felt childish and stupid doing it, even in my dream. It was vital I got through to them; I just couldn't stop this pathetic waving.

Hey, I shouted up at them. Dylan! Tanya! It's me, Jonathan.

This time all the different, but the same, versions of the two of them looked down and saw me. They were like a procession of weird dolls stuck up in the sky. They recognised me. Definitely. Looked briefly at each other as if they were deciding on something. And then they looked away.

A Bad Case of September

There used to be aviaries in Haulfre Gardens. There were cockatiels and Chinese finches, great flurries of canaries, and small green parrots that sat so still on their high perches they looked like carvings. Gone now, of course. Newly married, she'd brought Bob here to see her favourite view across to Shangri La, and to see the birds she'd loved as a child. Too late, even then. There were no long leafy oblong cages anymore, where she'd stand quietly to see, to listen, to enter a world of shrill squawks and whoops and gossipy background chatter. Gone long years ago.

In her new apartment at Avalon Court (how Bob would have sneered at that. Who d'you think you are now, he'd say. Morgana Le Fay?) in the second bedroom she hadn't really wanted but, what the hell, all the apartments had two bedrooms, so she'd turned it into her Room of Her Own for writing, she'd sat in front of the screen and tried to describe those birds. She saw all the letters of the words she typed assemble and disassemble, assume appropriate colours, appropriate movement, specific hops and glides. Swift, bright behaviours of wings were flickering in the screen's twiggy verbiage. She'd liberated them. Now her letter birds were free to sail above the lispy word of the isthmus on gentle thermals of the Indian summer's precisely poignant light.

Too bloody literary, said her dear, dead Bob. He'd become her internalised bullshit detector, ever ready to turn down any emergent eruptions of purple prose. But it wasn't all bullshit, was it? How often had her thoughts and opinions been subsumed into his? She'd let it happen, and let it happen contentedly, for the most part, sometimes with wry amusement, sometimes scarcely aware it was happening at all. Well, she was aware now. She still missed him, searingly sometimes, but she felt at the same time that she was beginning to spread her wings. Her own wings.

She suddenly found herself wondering what had happened to those birds in the winter. They were sheltered, she supposed, in the lee of the Great Orme, and in the gardens palm trees were growing still, so it must have been a place of mild winters. But some of those birds were surely delicate exotics. How did they survive? Were they taken somewhere else where there was heating for them? One thing was certain nowadays. Unless you had security guards on duty 24/7 you'd have all those hoodies taking pot shots at them with airguns. Kalashnikovs even. She had to smile then. Such hyperbole! Just listen to you, she said to herself. You're beginning to sound like Disgusted of Tunbridge Wells. Not surprising really. At Avalon Court she was surrounded by people Bob would have described as insufferably bourgeois. Mmm. Nobody accused anybody of being bourgeois now. It was a condition to which everyone aspired. Anyway, they weren't just insufferably bourgeois; they were insufferably English too. Judith had never thought of herself as militantly Welsh but too much exposure to her neighbours' twee surface politeness could bring her out in a nationalistic rash. Mind you, even here there were many and varied types and degrees of Englishness, revealed involuntarily in an occasional residual Brummie vowel or a hint of Scouse nasality. Had she made a mistake in moving here? She wasn't prepared to admit it, even if she had.

Llandudno held so many memories for her, all of them

good, and she couldn't have stayed on all alone in that echoingly empty house, could she? Here on the Promenade, with her view to die for, (well yes, wasn't that what they were all waiting for here, on the infamous Costa Geriatrica) she could still be stunned daily by the changing colours of sky and sea. She had security here, access on the flat to every-thing she needed and a lift to her apartment. So eminently sensible, this move, she'd thought. At her age, not that she was by any means decrepit yet, you had to look ahead. Her own variant on a theme of studied British reticence had held at bay those unappreciated neighbours but if she'd put up psychic barriers on the one hand, she'd reached out with open hands on the other. She'd enrolled on a twice-a-week Wlpan course to revitalise her Welsh and enable her to meet people who were, by definition, sympathetic to the language. Almost a knee-jerk reaction, that, to an encounter in the foyer where residents collected their mail. A certain Mrs Darlington was complaining about the waste of time and money involved in issuing bilingual utility bills. Judith had told her what she thought. Bob would have been proud of her. Perhaps what had annoyed her most of all was the automatic assumption that a resident of Avalon Court would be of the same anti-Welsh opinion. Bob's tone of voice, Bob's body language would have labelled her naive. She could hear him now, rebuking her. Come off it, girl, he'd have said. What did you expect?

Anyway her own attitudes to Welsh and Welshness, Bob's too, were, and had always been, complicated. They'd been brought up to speak Cymraeg Sir Fflint, and a smattering at that, and in the eyes of y boneddigion Gwynedd that placed them beyond the pale. Judith felt far more robust about her roots and her Welshness now, but her sense of linguistic inferiority had been all too destructively real. These were issues she'd intended to explore in the Creative Writing lessons she'd started attending a year ago, last September, just a couple of weeks after she'd moved to Avalon Court. It hadn't worked out like that. You weren't supposed to strike out on your own, though of course there was nothing to stop you examining your borderland consciousness for your own private satisfaction. Still, she'd enjoyed the classes, despite, at the start, having more than a sneaking suspicion that she would have made as effective a job of tutoring any day as Mandy, the sweet but slightly ditsy young woman who regaled them week by week with over-ingenious trigger exercises, and who, as far as Judith could make out, had never published anything herself. You really are getting bitchy, aren't you, she'd thought then. Good. Makes up for lost time.

As the course progressed, her admiration for Mandy had grown. They were a disparate bunch, decidedly mixed ability, you might say, and Judith was impressed by the way this smiling, deceptively innocent-seeming girl kept the peace, bringing out the shy and uncertain whilst maintaining a firm but amiable control of the more flamboyant types. This morning the course had reconvened for the new season, Judith noting, again with admiration, that all the former students bar one had turned up for more, along with three new faces. Their first homework was straightforward enough: My Dream Place. It could be real or imaginary. She filed the date, Friday September 29. Right, she thought.

Write! So here we go then, with:

Shangri La

*That's what my mother called our favourite view and I
thought that's what it was really called. Looking across
from Haulfre gardens, over the West Shore towards
Deganwy and the Conwy Estuary. Across the water the
mountains beyond the walled town and the castle seemed
so crisp and close. Sometimes they were misty or purplish
with heather, once they'd been invisible under thick rain-
clouds. It was years before I knew that you could climb
up from the town to the Sychnant Pass and then down
to Dwygyfylchi, and Penmaenmawr with its great
quarry and the huge clock on the hillside.*

Dwygyfylchi! Judith mouthed the word with delight. I'd love
to hear Mrs Darlington attempt to pronounce that. My
dear, she'd say (well, no, in all fairness she probably wouldn't
say any such thing. Still, for the purposes of this exercise...)
Extraordinary language. Quite absurd. Looks like Polish. No
vowels, you see. Something equally dismissive and ignorant,
anyway. You're letting this woman get under your skin, she
told herself. She's not important. No, but there are just too
many people with attitudes like hers. Especially here.
    Back to Shangri La.

*For me Shangri La was a kind of painted backdrop. I
never thought you could go there. It was like a magical
piece of the sky.*

She edited that immediately. Less prevarication with that
'kind of', she muttered mentally, and remember that
metaphor is stronger than simile. Get rid of that 'like'. That's
better.

For me Shangri La was a painted backdrop. I never thought you could go there. It was a magical piece of sky. By the time I found out that the term Shangri La came from James Hilton's novel, Lost Horizon, that it referred to some secret valley in Tibet and had entered the language as a shorthand term for any ideal, imagined place, I hadn't seen our special view from Haulfre Gardens for years. The summertime day-trips to Llandudno stopped when my mother fell ill. I was nine years old then. I was twelve when she died. Three years in the life of a child is an eternity. But my notion of Shangri La as that place across the water we never went to because it wasn't the sort of place you actually went to, it being too special for that, well, that stayed with me. Only it was no longer located visually, there on our horizon, ahead of us. It was behind us now. It moved out of space and into time. Past time. And it became imbued with sadness. And with loss. And the happiness and laughter my mother carried round with her all went away. To Shangri La. Mixed up with all the other memories. These were of the real places we really did go to, but looked back at now (and not just now: this paradoxical composite region of joy and loss, of imagination and reality, that for convenience's sake I'm dubbing Shangri La, was a constant retreat for me) they enter a different realm, are bathed in nostalgia's light. Real places become the stuff of legend, the focus of parable. Llangernyw. On the bus to Abergele and then turn left and climb, up past the chest hospital, down to Llanfairtalhaearn where we had a picnic once by the river; on again, along the loveliest windiest road beside the Elwy. And at Rhos Helyg there was Aunty G (short for Gwladys), and

Aunty Miriam. And their mother, old, old Aunty Sally. Who was nasty.

I'd been exploring in the garden and went into the coal place. It was next to the privy. The roof was broken a bit in one part, and the long tendrils of a blackberry bush had grown inside. There, just like a vine with grapes growing on it, just like the pattern round the words in my Llyfr Ysgol Sul, there, hanging down to tempt me was a single spray of blackberries, silhouetted against the pocket handkerchief of pale blue sky. Five of the fattest, juiciest blackberries you ever saw. And so special because of growing in the coal place. I was so excited. (She does get over-excited easily, doesn't she?)

I ran into the house, into the suddenly dark front parlour. I told them. I thought they'd be thrilled like me. Perhaps Aunty G and Aunty Miriam would've been thrilled if they'd had the chance. I know my mother would've been. We could have shared the blackberries. One each for the five of us. I wouldn't have dreamed of eating them all myself.

Don't you think you're having those, said old, old Aunty Sally. They're not for you.

I learned a valuable lesson that day. Having always been a child who tried desperately hard to be good becoming somewhat priggish, no doubt, in the process, I understood that some people stopped you doing things and having things out of sheer spite. Nothing but spite. Years later again I recognised that this spite was doubly delightful for the practitioner because, as well as the ego-boosting buzz derived by wielding power in denying a child, and the relish of reading its disappointment on its face, it carried with it the particular pleasure of simultaneously occupying the moral high ground. This was the exclusive territory of the self-righteous. Old, old Aunty Sally was one of the old, old school. It was in the child's interest to ensure it was deprived. It was good for that child's soul. Further, breaking a child's spirit was a sacred duty. Beatings were frowned upon now, for the most part, in these enlightened post-war days, so opportunities provided for child denial were becoming thin on the ground. No wonder she'd looked so pleased with herself. I'd offered her the twin kicks of sadistic satisfaction and moral justification at the same time. On a plate.

I realised old, old Aunty Sally hadn't got the faintest idea that there were blackberries growing in her coal place. I vowed there and then that if I ever found blackberries growing like that again, anywhere in the world, I wouldn't tell anybody. I'd eat them all myself.

Sometimes, in doing these writing exercises, Judith was surprised by the vehemence of her feelings. Inappropriate to feel angry about the old, old school now, surely. She stopped writing and looked out of the window. Somebody, it might have been Somerset Maugham, had said somewhere that a writer should always sit with his (note that personal pronoun) back to the window. Well she hadn't. This small bedroom had a view over the promenade and over the sea that was constantly interesting. One way or another. And she had no intention of wasting it. Right now, almost immediately opposite, a pair of grandparents (well, they were either oldish parents or youngish grandparents) were remonstrating with a couple of pre-school children. The younger one, a girl, suddenly decided to up the ante, entering into a quite alarming temper tantrum. Perhaps there were benefits to that old, old school of child-rearing after all. Why did the pendulum have to swing so forcefully from side to side? Why couldn't it hover moderately and gently in the middle? Judith knew damn well she'd never have dared to indulge in such practices, even with her generally easy-going mother. You just didn't. Anyway, this particular little rebel had now thrown herself on the ground and was giving a classic demonstration of the heel-drumming technique. Her brother, previously just as whiny and obstreperous, had decided that this was his opportunity to be The Good Child par excellence and was standing by looking smugly angelic.

It was at this moment an internal voice that must have been her own, but which nonetheless surprised her, said, with clarion clarity: Bob, you deprived me of my grandchildren.

There was not even a hint of response from the still-there-occasionally friendly shade that was Bob. Just silence. He was probably just as astonished at this outburst as she was. And then, since Judith invariably tried to be fair and always looked at both sides, she found that she was now firmly upbraiding herself for hypocrisy in this matter. Hadn't she spent last Christmas with Meryl and Jim in the Lake District in order to avoid the ritual family Christmas thing? And hadn't she moved from their old home and ensconced herself here partly at least as a way of telling Gareth and Co that Nain was independent now. Not an object of pity or a needy recipient of strained, dutiful visits but a person in her own right with a programme of her own. It all sounded a bit adolescent now, if an adolescence delayed by something getting on for fifty years. And she had, admittedly, seen them briefly in the Easter holidays when all four of them stopped off en route to a cottage they'd rented for a week in Llyn. She reckoned they'd just wanted to see her new place. Curiosity, if nothing else.

You've become a very cynical person, she told herself. But what is cynicism if not a defence mechanism, against, well, life, and all its tribulations? There's a festering comfort to be found in looking for ulterior motives and hidden agendas. But if you continue long enough in that direction all your joy goes out the window. You get all dried up. Bitter and twisted. And what good does that do you?

Enough of this. She saved and logged off. I'm going for a walk, she announced to the empty room. And I know where I'm going.

After the first novelty of having the lift at her disposal, Judith had decided to use the stairs to keep herself fit. Now, just as she stepped into the foyer, she heard the smooth swishy hum of the lift doors opening. Mrs Darlington stood there, leaning on a walking frame, her face for a moment unprepared for the world and especially unprepared for Judith. She looked old and tired and in pain. Just briefly. Equally, just briefly, Judith felt a surge of sympathy for her. Gone though, with disconcerting rapidity as soon as their eyes met. The cold hauteur that crossed the woman's face startled Judith. She thinks I'm a dangerous Welsh nationalist, she thought, a viper in the collective bosom of the English bastion that is Avalon Court, in the further all-engulfing English bastion that is Llandudno. Thank God for the Wlpan class, the last Welsh redoubt! She walked briskly in the direction of the pier, a sharp breeze blowing in straight off the sea. She felt uncomfortable. Perhaps she could have handled things a bit more diplomatically when they first had their, er, difference of opinion. Judith knew only too well that it was unlike her to take up the cudgels over anything really. She'd never had to. She'd always had Bob to do that. Her role had always been to placate and soothe. After the event.

The light was fierce now, a shrill wind rising. Almost October and autumn truly here. Judith's eyes stung. She was seeing something she hadn't seen before, or perhaps more honestly had never allowed herself to see.

So many events and emotions in her life had been lived almost vicariously. Her experiences were not so much her own as mediated through Bob, through Bob's experiences. These gushes of anger she kept feeling nowadays, about things currently happening, and things that had happened so long ago they ought to have long been irrelevant, were new to her. And frightening. It was Bob who had always expressed her anger, along with his own. What sort of person did that make her? Some kind of cipher? Her husband's mental clone? She realised that for much of the time recently she'd been floundering. Since Bob's death her personality had gone into hiding. Or was it that she'd never had a personality of her own? Bob had always been famously irascible. Sometimes half-jokingly. More often not. Her function, after the worst of his fulminating had subsided, was to agree, first of all, with his point of view. There was no cowed little wifey behaviour here, she hoped. No, their agreement on most topics was genuine. They saw the world from similar vantage points. They were in accord. Fine. It was just that she recognised now that in being the one who always took the heat out of things, by involving him in what was sometimes quite a complex process of acknowledgment and eventual acceptance, she'd constantly undergone a kind of mutual therapy alongside him. But he was part of that process. And now he wasn't here it was as if she wasn't here either. Meryl in Keswick, all those months back at Christmas, had suggested she went for some kind of bereavement counselling. Wise, subtle Meryl. It was just that back then Judith had still been in denial. It wasn't until she came here, to Avalon Court, that she realised quite how lost she was.

In her mind's eye she saw Mrs Darlington again, framed in the lift door, against the background of the quiet pastels of the foyer. And this time the anger came up again. Pure and clean. Her own anger. But I wasn't rude, she thought. I wasn't aggressive. She spoke to me first and, don't let's wrap it up, she was so blinkered and prejudiced. I was really quite reasonable, wasn't I? I was only reminding her that there were two languages in Wales after all. I didn't push it. Trouble is it's quite pointless trying to be reasonable with someone like Mrs Darlington. You can't reach someone like her. She'd never learn anything new. She'd never change. She was riddled through with outmoded notions of Empire and Englishness, their innate superiority, odious ideas in their heyday. Pathetic now.

Judith had walked a long way on automatic pilot. She'd intended to go to Haulfre Gardens before seeing Mrs Darlington, but after that, and after asking herself such probing questions, well, it seemed as if her feet had simply pulled themselves in that direction. She must have been paying attention to the other people on the pavement because she hadn't bumped into anybody and she must have been paying attention to the traffic when crossing the road, because she was still in one piece, but she'd been far too busy in her head to otherwise register her surroundings. Somehow she'd got as far as here, to the tram terminal. But these weren't the trams of the conventional variety, those large looming monsters that had thrilled and scared her as a child here in the fifties. No, this was the funicular railway station. What did they call it? Rack and pinion or something? Bob would've known. She'd actually walked right past Cae Gwylan, the boarding house she'd stayed at with her mother on their only ever night away from home. And her mother had chosen Cae Gwylan because it was a modest enough place and because it was also one of the very few B and B places actually to have a Welsh name.

She turned now and looked back down the street. It was all as vivid as if it had happened yesterday. There, at Cae Gwylan, she had learned two wonderful new words: funicular and curlicues. Those elaborate railings were still there, those whirly twirls painted white now. There, in the company of her new best friend of the moment, Cora, aged ten, she'd come across the shiny new concept of glamour. She was sitting on the warm stone step in the sun, Cora on the step above her. She'd never heard the name Cora before. What a beautiful name it was. Out of a window there floated bubbles of summer sound, Doris Day singing 'Que sera, sera'.

'...The future's not ours to see...' and a good job too, thought Judith. Who would have thought that shining day was to be one of the very last. That in less than a year's time her mother would be ill. Rephrase that. Dying. Slowly.

It was Cora's father who told her that the words 'que sera' were Italian, just as he told her, too, what funicular meant and what curlicues were. He was obviously a very clever man. Those are wrought-iron curlicues, he said. He was so very different from her own father back home. He looked so young for a start. He was young and smart and wearing a suit. He sported a quiff. A muted version of a teddy boy maybe. A bit of a wide boy too, possibly, though, as with 'glamour', she didn't know the word. Like Cora he wore interesting shoes. They were black and slender shoes, not winkle pickers exactly but not far off.

To wear them at all he must have had slender feet. The kind of feet that could dance. Judith had never considered the possibility of a man dancing. Or of a man having slender feet. Her father had big broad feet. He had his dusty working boots and he had his Wellington boots for when he went fishing. He had his slippers which were a kind of brown, grey and white tartan and he had his reddish brown leather laced-up shoes. And the laces were reddish brown too. Cora's father's shoes, she decided, were Italian. For a while, because que sera was Italian, curlicues and funicular became Italian words, too, and naturally Cora and her father were also Italian. So was Llandudno. It made sense. But because her mother must have been sitting in the lounge inside while she was having such an educational time outside with Cora and her father, all these new things never went into the nostalgia receptacle that was Shangri La. Her mother was the necessary ingredient to confer Shangri La status on something. It was so obvious, that, but Judith had actually never considered it before. There was a lot she hadn't considered before. She'd never asked herself where Cora's mother was. Or might have been, if she actually had a mother. Was she inside with her own mother? She didn't think so. She had no recollection of Cora having a mother at all.

Glamour, though, they had in bucketsful, these two, whoever they were. It was probably bargain-basement glamour, but that didn't bother the eight-year-old Judith. Innocent days. It was a necessarily brief infatuation. They were only there for the one night, Judith and her mother, that is, staying somewhere bed and breakfast for the one and only time because it would have been too late to get home from Llandudno following the concert the night before. Her mother had wanted to see Russ Conway playing the piano in the theatre.

Needless to say her father hadn't wanted to go, but at least he hadn't stopped their fun. Fair play. And, oh yes, this whole time, less than twenty-four hours of it, had been more glamorous than anything she'd ever known. She wondered, now, who they were, Cora *et père*. They couldn't have been well off or they wouldn't have been staying at Cae Gwylan. Even now, all these years later, Judith was still intrigued.

Other elements of Cae Gwylan remained so vital and fresh. The gong in the hall, rung with a splendid flurrying boom. It stood on an ornate stand with carved dolphins. The warming pan of polished brass and copper with a long wooden handle hung on the wall in the dining room above the long table where all the guests took their meals. No separate tables here. The strange almost pompous formality of the proprietress, which Judith, with no experience of irony, saw Cora's father send up with an exaggerated formality of his own. And a broad wink in her direction which she thought so funny and so brave. Outside again. Doris Day in the background. Cora with a butterfly slide in her hair. Unlike Judith with her solid sensible Start-rites she wore delicate black patent shoes, almost like ballet pumps but with a slim bar across the instep. Her socks, oh, what socks, white cotton ankle socks like Judith's own but transformed by a filigree, turned-over edge of scalloped lace. Socks to take the breath away...

Stop it, she told herself. You're doing it again. Digging up your precious (beautifully ambiguous word, that 'precious') eidetic images to divert and avoid. You've been doing it all your life. It's your device for setting up a whole philosophy of evasion. Give it a rest.

They are modest, unobtrusive gardens, Haulfre Gardens. I bet Mrs Darlington doesn't even know they're here, Judith thinks, feeling slightly guilty again, reminding herself that the poor woman wouldn't have been physically capable of climbing up here even if she had known of their existence. It's a steep pull up from Church Walks.

The self-effacing cousin of the Happy Valley (sounds like it ought to be a brothel in Hong Kong, Bob had said long ago), Haulfre Gardens are narrow and terraced, hugging the side of the great and wondrous lump of limestone that is the Great Orme. From the top the view's magnificent, of course. This view is different. You're not high up, and it's a closer, more intimate view, sideways on to the town. Beyond the fencing behind you Scots pines grow closely together, providing shelter. Beyond the little gate that opens onto a snaking path among gorse bushes the view widens out, takes in the whole of the estuary, and shines in the openness of flashing: wind and light.

In 2001, just a week or so after 9/11, when everyone still felt numb and strange (and shocked and awed, but as we know, that expression surfaced later, somewhere else) and the sky wore strange apocalyptic cloud streaks that were perfectly innocent and natural but didn't look it, she'd come here with Bob, and they'd stood where she stood now, looking down at the isthmus upon which had been constructed the elegant Victorian watering place that was Llandudno. Isthmus: a lovely lispy word indeed, and how vulnerable it all looked, this flat plain between two arms of the sea. Fears of global warming were in the air, mingling now with newly hatched and previously unimagined nightmares of terror. The Millennium celebrations seemed so far away, belonging to another age a mere eighteen months ago when there'd been optimistic dreams of new possibilities for the infant century. Well, they didn't last long. And nor had Bob. They'd had such plans. Nothing madly extravagant, just the idea of time together, really. To go to Italy again. To cruise the Norwegian fjords, maybe. Neither of them cared for sun and sangria and lounging on a beach. No thanks. But they did like the great cathedral cities. They liked the Peak District. They'd planned to go back to Ireland, to explore the Dingle Peninsula and the Burren, that horizontal limestone treasure. For a moment, all these things that might have been, hovered on the edge of a glorious receptacle, not unlike Shangri La. You're not going to do it again, Judith told herself. You're not going to do what you did with your mother, making a holy shrine for her in your mind, and living half your life in it. You were a child then. You weren't mature enough to do anything else. It was a kind of compensation for what was happening at home, where it was as if she had never existed. No one ever mentioned her once she was dead. Yes, that's the word. Dead. Not gone to heaven. Just plain dead. In that brief hovering moment Judith felt something happen. It was not a matter of intention or will. It happened of its own accord. The receptacle that was Shangri La ceased to be. It didn't smash into smithereens. There was no accompanying fanfare. It just went.

No more happy land with its own music, her mother's smile its leitmotif. And no more hiding the truth about her marriage. Bob was no saint. He could be selfish and cantankerous. He hadn't liked his daughter-in-law, and there was no good reason for his dislike. No excuse for it. That clarion call earlier. It was not the first time she'd heard it peal out a truth she didn't want to hear. At Keswick, at Meryl and Jim's, she'd seen how close they were to their grandchildren. And it hurt. She was so envious of their ease with each other, their warmth. I never really bonded with Lleucu and Haf, she thought. I never got the chance.

In view of Bob's downright unpleasantness, Shani would have been quite justified in never coming to see them at all. But she did. Over the years she'd endured stiff, tense Christmases for the sake of Gareth and the girls. When Lleucu and Haf were still quite small, Judith and Bob had twice rented a cottage down south, once in Pembrokeshire and once on the Gower. Gareth and Co had driven over to spend a few hours with them. Judith had told them they'd been staying there. Well, at least that meant there were two occasions when she'd stood up to Bob. It had taken a bit of doing, that. She should have done it more often. He hadn't wanted them to know, hadn't wanted to see them at all. She had bright pictures in her mind still, the lily ponds at Bosherston, splashing in the sea at Rhosili, but it was no thanks to Bob. He'd been sulky, sullen. Why? What was the matter with him?

If she was now in the process of pressing the delete key on some of her memories, especially those preserved in files labelled *Sentimental/Miscellaneous*, others, unbidden, were coming up for air. There was that conversation in the kitchen with Gareth, just the two of them, four, maybe all of five Christmases back. Is it because Shani's too Welsh for him? he'd asked her, exasperated yet again by his father's behaviour. Is that why he treats her like this?

Judith couldn't recall her reply. Something non-committal, no doubt. Some anodyne rubbish. But she remembered the expression on Gareth's face, a mixture of pain and anger, of incredulity and genuine puzzlement. But he'd hit the nail on the head, and she'd registered his observation's accuracy then, filing the knowledge away for future reference. Meaning now. Shani was too Welsh for him. Even as she herself had been all those years ago when they'd been so young and so in love. Not so much in love, mind you, that Bob didn't mock her for being just that little bit more Welsh than he was. Even if her Welshness was, like his, of the Flintshire variety. There were different degrees of Cymraeg Sir Fflint, it seemed. Bob certainly had the very best Flintshire credentials, being Shotton born and bred, with steel in his soul. You can't get more Flintshire than that. But perhaps it wasn't so much that Shani was too Welsh for him that brought out his ire in petty, spiteful ways that were unworthy of him. The problem was closer to home. In proximity to Shani, Bob became conscious of his own negative ethnicity. He was not Welsh enough. And it riled him, perhaps only on a half-conscious level. He thought of himself as Welsh. Of course he did. You only had to see him watching a Six Nations match to know that. There was no greater pleasure than to see England defeated. But in the Welshness stakes he was not *y peth go iawn*.

Perhaps it was only at college that Bob had come to realise the extent of his diluted and compromised Welshness. Judith had always known the score. As a fledgling eisteddfodwr of the variety that never got beyond the first prelims, she'd observed all those girls who walked away with the prizes. They were different. They spoke Welsh at home all the time, natural as breathing.

It was through the small Urdd group in her primary school that she and a few other hapless souls were put through their paces with the Unawd dan Naw and the Cân Actol. Waste of time. No contest. It was a farce really, though they'd enjoyed their eisteddfodau, if more as mini-anthropologists than serious competitors. The people around them were all fizzing and frothing with the splendid richness of their Welsh. They inhabited another world. Was it here that Judith had first learned to be a watcher rather than a joiner? If you couldn't belong you had to find something else to do, didn't you?

Detachment could be quite entertaining.

At least she and Bob had made sure Gareth would never be on the outside, as they'd been. They'd seen to it that he'd attended a Welsh medium school from day one, regretting that in their day education through the medium of Welsh was still in the early experimental stage, their own parents highly suspicious of it. Bob retained his customary scepticism. They'll move the goalposts now, you watch, he'd said. If you're in an exclusive club you don't want any bugger joining. Even he had been forced to admit, eventually, that things had changed, that there was a new inclusiveness. Up to a point.

Standing here, with the light percussion of dried palm leaves rattling incongruously in the wind beside her, Judith remembered all those eisteddfodau: the Miners' Institute at Ffynnongroyw, the Memorial Hall at Trelawnyd, the Lecture Hall at Capel Ebeneser, in Rhuddlan, where, if you slipped out to the shops in the High Street during the break you got stamped on your hand with a big purple label to show you'd already paid to get in. And she remembered one particular inglorious moment of her own when, unable to recognise the simple air Miss Harrison played for them, disguised now amongst all the trills and fol-de-rols of the official accompaniment, she'd insisted, to much consternation, that this was not her tune. The accompanist had very helpfully transposed the 'tune' up and down the keyboard with increasingly exasperated flourishes, but to no avail. Miss Harrison was red in the face.

Just at this moment, below her, there were suddenly children's voices. The infants section of a school down there had closed for the day, shrill, excited piping filling the air, mingled with the murmur of mothers and the distant revving of engines. Judith felt her legs go wobbly. She walked to the far end of the garden, to the bench in that little protected niche near the gate leading on to the Orme. A withered wreath lay there, recalling the life of someone who had probably once loved this place as much as she did, someone who even remembered the aviaries, maybe. She sat down gratefully, feeling suddenly old, as if she'd had a premonition of what really being old meant, breathless, unsteady on one's feet, uncertain of one's thoughts, unsure of who one was. At least Bob had been spared all that.

Behind her, framed under the graceful, almost mannered curve of the lowest branch of a Scots pine, was the view across to Shangri La. She didn't want to look at it. The wind had tossed the sound of the children's voices out of range. Well, this really was a bad case of September. That had always been a favourite phrase of Bob's in the first week or so of every new school year. He had this belief that the summer holidays were too long. Not that he didn't enjoy them. He did. It was just that he reckoned, and this was something to do with biorhythms, that following six weeks plus of freedom, kids and teachers alike were so wrenchingly affected by the re-imposed discipline of school routine that the process of adjustment was unnecessarily painful. The holidays shouldn't last so long. Your holiday didn't last long, did it, Bob? Again she ached for him, warts and all. People's vices were so often the flip side of their virtues, weren't they? And Bob had had plenty of virtues. What you saw with him was always what you got. Nothing hidden. Nothing sly. All his awkwardness, all his bloody mindedness, were part of his radical honesty. It made him enemies as often as it made him friends. It had made him the man she loved.

I'll phone Shani when I get home, she thought, with sudden clarity. She was surprised she'd thought of that word. Home.

Not when I get back. No, when I get home. Because that's what Avalon Court was now. I'll play it by ear. I'll say I'm sorry things were as they were. I'll try to explain. It's a bit late, admittedly, to make amends. To put it mildly. But if it doesn't work at least I'll have tried. They asked me to go and stay with them after Bob died, and churlishly I said no. Thank you, but no. If the offer's still open I think I'd like to say yes.

The light was fading from the sky and it was getting colder, as if the wind had changed direction. She pulled her coat closer. If sea levels rise to any serious extent there won't be any Llandudno at all, she thought. In a hundred years or thereabouts the sea might be lapping at the foot of the Great Orme here, below me, and across the bay too, at the foot of the Little Orme. And in between there'll be nothing but water. Goodbye isthmus.

She gulped and shivered. She was cold and stiff, and felt suddenly exhausted. Behind her the great mineral heart of the Orme was suspended between beats of geological time. A fanciful notion, Bob would have deemed that, but she was allowed the occasional fanciful notion on his behalf. He'd become an increasingly keen botanist in recent years and had looked for spiked speedwell on the slopes immediately above the gardens. He'd never found it. Perhaps in the Burren he'd have discovered his elusive limestone flower. Don't get soppy, girl, the air around her said.

Just then a slight movement above her head, a real live breathing goldcrest, stitching its way between the selvedges of branches and needles and small green cones. She held her breath. It made its way so delicately along the branch, scrutinising the surface of the bark for insects; tiny, fearless, the perfection of its feathers almost tangible. It had no illusions about its identity. It didn't know whether it was a Welsh goldcrest or an English goldcrest. It didn't even know it was a goldcrest. I've undergone a sea change, Judith felt, though the feeling was beyond words, as was the sense in her blood and in her bones of the sheer insubstantiality of everything.

Messages

Beyond concepts, this cedar tree is simply and perfectly itself. Today I'm seeing it for the last time. After two years of false starts and rumours, Highbrake is finally closing. On Monday staff and residents will bundle into cars, making a small and poignant convoy as they drive just a few miles down the road to the new purpose-built unit. It stands in the same grounds as a day centre and a clinic. No cedars there. I just hope Sean won't be any trouble. He told me a while back that on the day Highbrake closed for good, he'd set off on his own and no one would be able to stop him. No one would ever find out where he'd gone either. The idea pleased him. He sat back in his chair, his hands clasped behind his head, and he looked downright smug. I saw him as a Dick Whittington figure trudging down a country lane with all his belongings tied up in a spotted scarf slung on a stick. Ridiculous that: Sean would never go anywhere without all his atlases and all his maps, and he'd need a supermarket trolley to carry them.

You don't actually think we'd just let him disappear into the blue yonder, do you? Dr Hansen looked at me severely, puzzled it seemed, even offended.

But how can you stop him if he's not on a section? I asked. He knows his rights, and he's here voluntarily.

Only theoretically, he said.

But the story begins twenty-two years ago. Sean was seven. I was nine. Our mother had been admitted to Highbrake the day before and here we were, visiting. It was bright October.

Here was Sean, busily filling his pockets with conkers under the big horse chestnut tree. Here was I, on the same spot exactly that I'm standing now, across the car park and a piece of thin grass, falling under the protective spell of the cedar tree. I had never seen such a tree. I looked up into its silence and stillness. I did not know what the word symmetry meant but I was responding to its meaning nonetheless, as I stood below in its calm shadow and saw how its branches echoed each other on each side of the great furrowed trunk. It seemed to me that this trunk, its solidity, the sequence of strong patterns on its bark, its sheer hugeness, was somehow all part of a message I could not understand. But that didn't matter. On one level, a level without words, I understood that message. I think I fell in love with the cedar tree.

This was the first time our mother had been admitted to Highbrake, but it was not as if she'd suddenly become ill. When you're a kid you take what's happening around you as normal, and for us it was normal to have a mother who spent most of her time in bed, hardly speaking to us, crying sometimes, making a soft low keening sound like a cat that's been trapped in a shed. Sometimes she'd be different; warm, funny, telling us stories, laughing uproariously at her own jokes, buying us expensive presents she couldn't afford, talking very fast and ever faster, flirting with the milkman, the postman, and once, memorably, shocking two freshfaced earnest young Mormons who'd turned up on the doorstep to convert her. They couldn't get away fast enough.

After the laughter and the expansiveness, which we'd come to dread, came the next, ultimately terrifying stage, as she herself became terrified. Of everything. Of us. Of our patient, well-meaning father. Of people passing the house. People she knew. People she didn't. Of a twig tapping on the window.

Of a starling on the coalhouse roof. Of the sound of the refrigerator, its low hum and the hidden message in it.

Messages. It seemed to me living was all about messages.

But I was the nervous one, wasn't I, the one who was highly strung. Sean was a lad, a real lad, and seemingly uncomplicated. He was fine, surely. No worries there. Sporty, physical, well co-ordinated, spontaneous. Not a bit shy. If anyone was fated to inherit my mother's mental problems it was bound to be me. As the years went by I took this for granted. My mother heard messages in the hum of the fridge, didn't she? I sensed them all around me. But I realise now that there was a crucial difference. My mother's messages came in words. She understood them all too well, consequently she never shared them with us. In her way, I'm sure, she was trying to protect us from them, those terrible messages that crushed her with the knowledge in them. My messages did not come in words. I didn't even begin to understand them. I didn't even try. But they were benign, I think, my messages.

Beyond concepts, the cedar tree is simply and perfectly itself.

We called them, retrospectively, The Troubles. Funny that, when you consider how our lives had never been without trouble of some kind. Still the problems with Sean were new, and shocking. So totally unexpected. He went from an easy-going eleven year old to a paranoid and violent twelve year old. It was as if someone had flipped a switch.

Where does it start, exactly? How do I pinpoint the change? Well, it surely must have begun with moving to the High

School. He hated it. He'd moved from a tiny rural school that was like an extended family, to a huge impersonal monster of bustle and noise. In the third week he decided he'd had enough. He wouldn't go. More than that, he wouldn't get out of bed, and heaven knows he'd had years of exposure to that particular problem solver. Not that it solves any problems at all. In the end.

My father had already left for work. It was up to me and my mother to attempt to get Sean off to school. It was hopeless. We managed to roll him out of bed but he lay rigid and immobile on the floor. We tried to get him dressed, pulling off his pyjamas with great difficulty, trying to ease on his clothes, lifting his arms, lifting his legs. My mother started to cry tears of rage and helplessness. Meanwhile Sean just lay there, not condescending to struggle with us, just opting out altogether. I'm sure he already had recourse to his own world, his own private mental structure, the place he would eventually live in, inaccessible to all of us. But not quite yet. Now came the long months of intervention: social workers, a child psychiatrist. He did start going to school again, but only to register in the morning and then disappear. He'd hang round town for a while, then make his way home over the fields. He sank his school bag and his books in a ditch, arriving back in the afternoon, muddy and bedraggled. He looked different. He'd grown so fast, yes, but this was something else. He had a wild look, his always dark eyes black now, the pupils so dilated. But there was one day I'd never forget. The day that changed everything.

It was a day in early May, summer suddenly following a wet spring. I remember the mud of the path slick underfoot, the white shine and glisten of wild garlic in the wood, that oniony smell sharp on the air. And I remember the fear. What he'd told me, I didn't believe he'd done, but I was afraid of the fact that he seemed to really think he'd done it. I felt already that this wasn't just macabre make-believe, that somehow things had already gone beyond a line, a boundary, separating the difficult but still just about ordinary from the dangerously crazy. I was going to prove to him that it wasn't how he thought, clinging to the idea that you can change someone else's thoughts by producing contradictory evidence. I was being so utterly reasonable. What a fool I was. But how could I know, then, that by definition a delusion is an unreasonable idea that no amount of reasoning can shift.

He told me that he'd stampeded a herd of cows into the river. That they were all in calf and that one of the cows had panicked and had fallen and was lying in the river and was going to drown. That it was in the process of giving birth and the calf was going to drown too. His words came out in a stampede of their own. I looked at him. This wasn't a wind-up. He really believed it. And it was up to me to prove to him that it wasn't true.

We went down the path to the Mound, a favourite place for children to play, the spot which had once boasted a Norman motte and bailey castle. There was the river, as quiet and peaceful as I'd expected it to be, with Friesians grazing contentedly on the far bank.

I turned to him. There you are, Sean, I said. Everything's alright.

Oh no it's not, he said. You're like all the others. You're all the same.

He looked at me with what I can only describe as sheer malevolence. But it was desperation really. He lashed out at me, hitting me, then kicking wildly. I put my arms up to protect my face.

I want more, he said. More. More.

More what? I said, trying to avoid the worst of the on-slaught, still trying to be reasonable, the sensible big sister, the troubled little brother. I wanted so much to make this right. Whatever it was he wanted I'd have got it for him. I'd have done anything.

I hate all of you. All of you. You none of you know anything. You're all so fucking stupid.

His rage was terrifying. His blows and kicks got fiercer, wilder. Instinctively I knew I mustn't fall, that I had to stay on my feet. And then I saw two people coming towards us across the field. A man and a woman, middle aged. Wearing cagoules and walking boots. History types, we called them.

Stop it, Sean, I said. Look, there's people coming. You've got to stop it.

And he did.

I didn't tell my parents. I kept my bruises to myself. Quiet days followed, and then he said to me, sheepishly, I've been round the bend, haven't I Shona?

You're alright now, I said.

But he wasn't.

I could catalogue Sean's downward spiral. I won't. I don't think I could bear to. Suffice to say that the next few years were like living in a horror film. It was nightmarish and it was pitiful. Hope can actually be very cruel. There were times when he was more, well, normal, but they were short-lived. The one thing I can't understand is that the medical powers-that-be insisted on calling it behavioural problems. We who lived with him knew it was more, and worse than that. There were so many psychotic episodes we lost count. Once two young policemen turned up, called by our next-door neighbours following one of Sean's more public demonstrations. He'd got on the garage roof and from there, armed with the prop for the washing line he managed to break all the windows at the back of the house.

Is he schizophrenic? one of the policemen asked. But he'd seen the worst of it. The doctors never did. Sean was usually able to give a brief good impression.

A few weeks after his eighteenth birthday he was finally diagnosed. Over a period of nearly six hellish years he'd never been given so much as a single Valium.

I've been thinking about the whole concept of family. What exactly is a family? It's not just a collection of people who live under the same roof. It's an energy system and sometimes that system goes wrong. Some sort of pathological energy focuses on one person, expresses itself through one person. For years, for us, this person had been my mother. Then, following her first stay at Highbrake, when at last she was medicated and monitored, her mood changes stabilising, all that bad energy had to find someone else to inhabit. That person was Sean. I know there's nothing scientific about this, and I know it could probably all be explained away as a matter of faulty group dynamics. I still cling to this idea of interconnected energy patterns, though. For me it makes some sort of sense.

There's a reason for all this introspection, this attempt to disentangle our history. You might imagine that when your mother's a manic depressive and your brother's a chronic schizophrenic, well, you might just come to the conclusion that it would be wise not to have children yourself.

I decided I would never have children. When I got married James accepted this and understood. But there's a world of

difference between deciding not to have children in the
abstract, and actually terminating a pregnancy, when, despite
all your precautions, somehow pregnant is what you become.
Perhaps I was just a fatalist at heart. Perhaps this was meant
to be.

James tried to put it in perspective.

You're alright, aren't you? he said.

What he meant was that I was adequately sane. And what he
was implying was that a child of mine would not necessarily
become mentally ill, that it wasn't inevitable.

It's still a risk, I said.

He looked at me. It's a risk every time you step out the
front door.

Why was Sean so ill, when I was ok? Was it just the luck of
the genetic draw? There were so many questions and there
were no satisfactory answers to any of them, as far as I could
see. I'd thought for a time that perhaps it was something to do
with my being so much a plodder. Sean had had such flair.
Charisma, if you like. He stood out. He was different. Me, I
plodded along, never drawing attention to myself, working
hard at school because it gave me a kind of security when I
needed all the security I could get. But I'd always dreamed
that there was a place somewhere for Sean. A special place,
an ideal environment where he'd prosper and thrive, where
in order to preserve his essential self he wouldn't have to
be psychotic. Or was that just a romantic evasion of what
schizophrenia really was?

I'd watched a documentary once about some rare and, it
has to be said, rather stupid flightless parrots in New Zealand.
Conservationists got some eggs incubated and reared the
chicks by hand and then they went up in a helicopter with
them to some remote island, all misty and forested. The young

parrots were fitted with microchips so their whereabouts could be traced. All this time and trouble for a few peculiar birds that were really blips on the great progressive journey of evolution. (That was irony by the way.) But I'd found the film moving, I have to admit. There was something strangely lovable about these slow green creatures with their funny stubby wings and their strange feathers, overlapping semicircles, the shape of fish scales. I wished them well in their new home, wishing at the same time that something similar could be done for Sean. Perhaps he could be a shaman in a tribal society somewhere. Perhaps in a conveniently Earth-like planet in another galaxy he could come into his own. Then I realised I was still putting my younger brother on a pedestal. It wasn't enough for him just to be well. He had to be special too. Why did I still think like this? Perhaps because he was frozen at puberty, had never developed from the disturbed twelve year old whose dreams were too extreme, too all engulfing and unfathomable ever to be realised, whose imagination was turned inside out and upside down by its own unregulated power.

And now I was about to let something happen. James was very reassuring but I knew, nonetheless, that I was about to take the greatest risk of my life. I knew the child I was expecting was a girl. And I knew what we would call her. Rebecca.

Becky. I hope love will be enough.

I was very glad to go to work today, to be able to get stuck into invoices and bills of sale, orders for baling wire and corrugated sheeting. Today was the day of the move. Even on Saturday Sean had still been in denial about the whole thing. I'd said something suitably bland about the new place, how nice it was with its ensuite rooms etc. He just looked at me with the cold, distant expression that tells you the subject is closed.

Once I got back home today my curiosity and apprehension got the better of me, and I just had to phone to find out if everything had gone according to plan. I wanted to make sure he really was safely transplanted in his new abode.

Everything's gone very smoothly, said Angela, Sean's been fine. All along he simply hasn't wanted to know, even when all the other residents went to look round the place. This morning, though, he was ready first thing, with all his maps and atlases in bags and boxes by the door.

He'd want to make sure none of then got left behind, I said.

They've all been safely delivered, she said. It's a funny thing I've noticed before with other residents, once they're sectioned it seems to calm them. Gives them a feeling of security.

What, I asked, incredulously. You mean he's been sectioned. When?

It must be a month, five weeks ago. A Section Three. That's for six months...

I felt like saying, thank you, Angela. I know what a Section Three is. I couldn't believe this. Why hadn't I been told? For a start, wasn't it a legal requirement for the next of kin to be informed? I said all this, keeping my voice measured and even, when I was really angry. All this worry I'd had for ages, so frightened that Sean would live up to his boast that he would indeed disappear into Dr Hansen's proverbial blue yonder.

We thought you knew, said Angela. And we definitely wrote to you.

What made him suddenly sectionable anyway? I asked. It's not as if his mental condition's deteriorated recently. Then I heard what I was saying. Why was I coming out with all this? I was glad he'd been sectioned. It meant that even if he had decided to go walkabout they would have been empowered to bring him back. I just wish I'd known earlier, that's all.

I was giddy with relief and exhaustion and I just couldn't sleep. I lay there quietly, listening to the ebb and flow of James' breathing, wondering whether I'd give up on the idea of sleep altogether, and go downstairs to make a cup of tea. When I tried to get out of bed, though, my legs felt so desperately heavy I couldn't make the effort to move.

And then the strangest thing happened. I wonder if somehow I'd managed to half-hypnotise myself as I lay staring hard at the weave in the textured linen-effect of the curtain, the glow of the street light exposing the grid pattern of warp and weft. Whatever caused it, for the first time ever in my life I had an out-of-body experience.

In the no-man's land between sleep and wake I found myself floating, literally floating along the road to Highbrake. Now that there was no reason for me to ever go along this road again, I felt a strange nostalgia for it. It was winter. The fields on the right were white with frost and on the left stood the complex of buildings we'd always known as The Main, the old Victorian mental hospital, empty for years now. As a child it had scared me stiff but I also found it fascinating. It looked to me just like a sinister French chateau in a picture book. Normally you could see the soft blue greens of the hills beyond but today a kind of radiant fog hung behind the roofs like a backdrop. The whole scene looked painted and artificial, the pinnacles and turrets silhouetted as if cut out of black cardboard.

There was the central tower, denuded now of its great

clock. I remembered my mother telling me how she lay sleepless at night up there in Highbrake, waiting for that icy bell to chime the hour. I felt I could hear it, a sound that was shiny and tinny and cold. But in its own way beautiful.

I think I could have quite happily continued to float above the road for ever, but then I heard noises: wails and whispers and the ceaseless twittering of human voices. Slowly, I realised what these voices were. I was listening to the stories of all the people who had been inmates of the hospital, going right back to its earliest days, well over a hundred years ago. Their stories had never been told, and they wanted them told. I felt the pressure of a great energy of frustrated expression rising up from the old walls. They wanted me to tell their stories. They wanted the record put straight. How can I tell your stories? I said. There are too many of you.

There must have been thousands of them. The air was full of their aural hieroglyphics, their unbearable music. Here were their lives as lived. Here were their lives as they might have been lived. I am not an imaginative person. All I have ever allowed myself to imagine are the parallel universes I concocted for Sean. But here was a multitude of pain lives and hope lives combined, represented by a kind of swirling movement that kept switching itself on and off, a dance of misery, a dance of impossible alternatives.

Eye of Battle

I feel more relaxed about it now but for most of my life I was ashamed of my background. As a kid, a runty, scrawny lad, a good three inches shorter than all the others in the class, I felt as if I was writhing in my own sense of inferiority. Mind you just about everyone else agreed I was inferior. At home, the youngest of six, I was ignored if I was lucky. At school I was bullied. The teachers seemed to take their cue from the worst of the kids. The only thing I had that was precious was my imagination.

At night I would lie in bed and enter my other place. It was by the sea. There was a narrow valley and in it a stream that flowed down to a pebbly shore. I liked the way the water thinned out into threads among the stones.

Home is not always where we live. We can make it elsewhere. Sometimes an imagined place is made flesh for us; it is walking into a dream, too real for firmness so we pinch ourselves to test ourselves awake. And then, when the place is proven, we can breathe its air, assuming all those colours we always knew were ours, birthright and mark.

Where my dream place had come from I had no idea. Was it from some tv programme I'd seen? From pictures in a travel brochure? My sister Carol worked in a travel agency and sometimes brought stuff home, but my secret valley by the sea was a very specific place and as unlike those generic pictures of white sands and palm trees as you could get. There was nothing Caribbean about my place. It seemed home-grown. Anyway, it never occurred to me that it actually existed. It was make-believe and I accepted it as such. Even so I'm sure it kept me sane.

As the years went by my dream place developed. I explored inland, following the stream to a kind of open green area where the sandy banks were replaced by an oak wood and a rocky outcrop. On it there stood a building of grey stone, a lookout tower, I thought, guarding the shore. I never met any people in my place, but there were birds and animals. Best of these were the deer. I would sit quietly in my hidden place up among the trees and wait for them to appear. I would watch my imaginary deer in my imaginary land until I fell asleep.

Then, when I was ten, in the next-to-top-class in primary school, Alan appeared.

Very few new kids ever came to our school and very few left. If you look at old school photographs that's what strikes you immediately. No one comes. No one goes. The reason for that's pretty simple. Who'd want to move into a rundown inner city area like ours? Plenty of people would have liked to move away but how could you do that with no money, and no prospect of a better job somewhere else? But then, suddenly, an old church on the corner of our street was converted into a community centre. There was a meeting place for old people, a youth club, a young mothers' drop-in and crèche. Did it make that much difference? I can't speak for anyone else but it made all the difference to me.

Quite a few people were employed at the centre, most of them part-time, but the full-time warden lived on site in a purpose-built flat. His name was Phil. His wife was called Esme and his son was called Alan. And Alan became my friend.

It was an ordinary Monday morning halfway through the Easter term. I honestly can't remember anyone new ever joining our class ever before, but suddenly there's the teacher introducing this kid and telling him to sit next to me. The only empty desk was the one next to me and it was empty because no one else wanted to sit in it.

Six weeks or so later I was on my first-ever holiday, with a group of boys from the newly formed youth club. We were camping by the sea in north Wales on land adjacent to a holiday village owned by Alan's uncle. By this time we were best friends, Alan and me.

Camping in the sloped field, you can see the tents, like pale cones, the moon a flurried dinner plate peeping out through a ragged cloth and the dawn rain making small speech against tarpaulin.

Remember the dream in the bell tent? How you woke and felt a pain thinning out in the drenched grass, how in that urgent disorientated moment you clutched the sleeping bag's lining in the dark that is somehow not as unfamiliar as you thought and not quite dark anyway, a misted place where the lined shapes are the sleeping bodies of the others, and a dog barks a question, tethered at the farm, and you see, as the zip of the sleeping bag catches your chin and a cool bead of blood inches down, a trace of a river (how is it made against the shadowy inside of the tent?) a meander, limping water, bayou still, that is neither a memory nor a portent but something that curls out of the corner of your sleep. In this time that perches between day and night and now and history you see, no, you almost are, an army of banners, the air taut with the nervousness of horses, chevrons of coots on the tidal bend, listening stillness, a clash of waiting.

That's what did it. Listening stillness. A clash of waiting. That's what changed me. As if all that latent, pent-up energy transferred itself to me. What was it anyway? Not a product of my imagination surely. Doesn't imagination have to involve some kind of intent? It just doesn't happen to you like that. You have to at least half make it happen, half want it to happen.

I wrote that account of the dream in the bell tent, much later for Sara. I write that name now and ask myself whether I miss her. Yes. It's years ago and I still miss her. But I don't regret the fact that she went out of my life. Paradoxical? Maybe. Anyway, as she pointed out at the time it wasn't a dream. We use that word loosely. It can mean different things. It certainly wasn't a dream in the sense of being something you experience when you're asleep. I wasn't asleep. It was a hypnagogic state, said Sara, and I can hear her voice as she says it. That light quick speech, the tone so often overlaid with irony. And that makes me think of Mr Pepper in his cluttered shop picking up a black filigree tray, holding it to the window to catch the light. It was always shadowy in his shop and he didn't like to waste electricity. Mean? In some ways yes, in others very generous. A paradox again. Interesting people, interesting situations. So often paradoxical. Indian, he says, handing the tray to me. Beautiful work that. Inlaid with ivory. Would you like it?

I can't believe it. This, for me? Just a kid? The first beautiful thing I'd ever owned. I take it home and hide it.

Fast forward again. Sara. Quirky, impulsive, the most emotionally independent woman I've ever known with a gift for life that left me breathless, an everlasting student with a genuine intellectual interest in just about everything. Are they extinct I wonder, in these days of fund it yourself? She was a post-grad literature student, her doctoral thesis a strange mutant gallimaufry on Literature and the Imagination. All was grist to her mill, though the main writers she was studying seemed to be Coleridge, Wallace Stevens, Borges and Ursula le Guin, all generously steeped in Carl Gustav Jung and his Collective Unconscious.

I knew nothing about any of this stuff but her enthusiasm for it all was infectious. She had this fervent belief that the power of the human imagination was colossal, potentially, but terribly neglected and undeveloped. In her eyes the education system stopped kids developing their imagination, so I asked her, straight out, how did she know?

How do I know what? she said.

How can you possibly know what a child's imagination is like? How can anybody know what goes on in a child's head? For all you know an apparently dull ordinary kid might have a rich imaginative life you know nothing about. And what goes on in school might have no effect on it whatsoever, one way or another. As far as I'm concerned education and imagination are totally unconnected. She looked at me quizzically. Hey, she said, that's quite an impassioned speech.

You mean coming from me?

She shook her head with exasperation. Why are you always so defensive? You always think I'm trying to get at you.

To prove what I meant, to show that a dull ordinary kid, namely me, could have a rich imaginative life I told her about my imaginary place by the sea. And how I found it. In real life. And how, as if that wasn't enough, when I was already reeling with the effect of that, something else happened that made me believe that, perhaps, in some places time wasn't linear at all, but circular. Cyclic. That certain events could be on some kind of loop, repeating themselves for ever. And it was possible, sometimes, don't ask me how or why, to access

events in the past, live in them, almost. Or somehow caves-
drop on them.

Ok I can accept most of that, she told me.

What can't you accept?

That you were ever a dull ordinary kid in the first place.

By now, in school, thanks to Alan, I had new improved status.
I was able to bask in the glow of his novelty, such a rare
commodity for all of us. Thanks to his association with the
community centre, which was the most exciting thing that
had happened around here since the Blitz (so I was told)
everyone wanted to know him. I was included in his halo
effect because Alan wanted me there. I couldn't believe my
good luck. At the start he must have been made aware that I
was at the very bottom of the pecking order, but it didn't
bother him. Was that because he was just a straightforwardly
decent kid, or was it because he rather liked having an adoring
sidekick? I had tried to hide the adoration bit, knowing it was
the antithesis of cool. I knew what cool was. Theoretically. Just
as I knew that I'd never acquire it, except perhaps by proxy,
like this.

The prospect of the proposed camping holiday by the sea
got us into a collective paroxysm of anticipation. Now that's
got to be Sara's influence. The pre-Sara me would never have
used an expression like collective paroxysm. Now don't blame
me, she'd have said. Just because I've got a wide vocabulary
doesn't mean I approve of verbosity. I couldn't win with Sara
and that was fine by me.

Eddie, the father of one of the boys, was going to drive a
minibus with room for twelve kids and a load of equipment,
while I was going to be one of the chosen few travelling in
Phil's car with Alan. He sat in the front with his dad and there

were three of us squeezed in the back. Only I, though, had the status of Best Friend. I had never been so far away from home, and in this I was not unusual. None of us had. Today was, no contest, The Best Day Of Our Lives.

We arrived early in the afternoon. We'd all brought sandwiches and we sat to eat them in fitful sunshine on benches in front of the small clubhouse. And then, with all our paraphernalia being trundled along on a couple of trolleys we made our way through the tidy rows of caravans and wooden chalets to the field where we'd pitch our tents. At the top of the field it was quite level, a stream flowing in from higher ground to our left, where farm buildings perched on a precarious looking edge. Then the land sloped down steeply between gently wooded banks to the sea. I couldn't believe my eyes. There was my tower. Just as it was in my imagination and had been for so long, night after night. I looked around me with a sense of something almost like fear. It couldn't be true. This couldn't be my place. Slowly I turned in each direction, comparing every detail. There were some differences. There were fewer trees for a start. The stream was less wide and less deep. And then I realised something. Here, now, in this real place, it was early summer. In my imaginary place it was always late autumn. Or thereabouts. I'd never actually considered that before, just taking the perpetual season for granted. The trees were always almost bare, the few remaining leaves brown or a crinkled rusty orange. There was always a wind blowing in from the sea, with just a hint of ice in it. What had I been wearing? I found myself wondering stupid things like that. I'd never felt cold, though I realised now that logically I should have done. Logically? When I'd actually been in my bed back home? I didn't know then, aged ten, what the word logical meant. But I knew I was up against something very peculiar. Scary peculiar. There was nothing logical about this. Solid earth was real and hard beneath my feet as I felt a sudden wrenching dislocation, reminding myself that I'd never really been here before.

It was my imaginary place that felt real, though, not this actual here and now.

And then Alan was shouting and tugging at my arm. With Phil and Eddie telling us what to do, we started to pitch the tents. I don't think I could have been much use. There was too much going on in my head.

Did you tell him that it was your place? Sara asked. How you'd been there before in your imagination?

Not straight away, I told her. I didn't dare. I thought he'd think I was making it up. There was more to it than that. It was more than my usual defensiveness. I hardly believed it myself, so how could I expect him to? Long years of experience had taught me caution and prudence. I knew it wasn't a good idea to step out of line. I was actually surprised to hear myself telling Sara about it now, all these years later, but she was different. By definition. And I was an adult, successful, affluent. Success and affluence enable you to step out of line. Or was it stepping out of line that had made me a rich somebody instead of an impoverished nobody in the first place? All these chicken and egg questions had been going round in my mind for quite a while. I'd recently allowed myself the luxury of thinking for its own sake, rather than thinking of ways to make money.

I'd been born in 1967, slap bang in the middle of the Summer of Love, a squalling accident of a baby in a back street on a planet going deliciously crazy with the notions of Making Love not War. Not that there was much in the way of California dreaming or wearing flowers in your hair where I hailed from.

By 1979, when Thatcher got elected, I was thirteen. In High School and coming out of my shell. Alan was still my friend. Even after I'd told him about the way his uncle's camping field was my imaginary place. I'd waited for the right moment, almost a year later. He hadn't thought me crazy. He hadn't thought I was lying. He just listened quietly. By now we'd stayed there again, but not camping with the youth club kids. Just us. In the flat above the clubhouse, with the family. I got to meet Janine, Alan's cousin. She was to be my first girlfriend actually, but that was later. In the meantime I'd grown. Physically. You're shooting up like a beanpole, Mr Pepper said, one morning as he opened the shop. Mentally, too, thanks to him, to some extent. but mostly thanks to Alan. Horizons I hadn't known existed began to expand. Emotionally? At the end Sara could have said I was still as emotionally stunted as ever.

Whatever, I'd begun to spread my wings. I began to feel that maybe I had a Midas touch: a kind of magic. And this time I told no one at all. Not even Alan. My imagination had taken a very different turn. I'd made up my mind that I wanted to make money. Lots of it.

And I did. All of which, in a roundabout way, brought me to a rather chi-chi new wine bar called Crusoe's. My wine bar. My latest toy. I'd got the best interior decorators money could buy to kit it out. The best manager to run it. I liked to think of myself as a bit of a promoter by now, so I got the best indie bands and the best solo artists to perform there. Though I say it myself we were briefly (these things are brief and then you move on) cutting edge.

And it was here I met Sara. She didn't know then that I owned the place.

Our relationship lasted just over two years, though for the last few months of that Sara was in a private clinic. I paid for her being there, nothing but the best, out of a kind of guilt really, though I'm jumping ahead of myself now. During all this time I'd lived in my apartment on the Salford Quays where she'd join me sometimes at weekends. Our lives were still largely separate. This suited both of us. She shared a big rambling rundown house with three other girls, two of them post-grad students like herself, the other a viola player in the Halle. We had our own circles and we did our own thing. With all the other women in my life (now that sounds like I was some sort of Casanova – not true) there'd always come the point when they wanted commitment. I dreaded that word. It meant the end. Everything I'd ever worked for was to give me space and freedom. I was a private person, self-contained. I liked company but I liked it on my terms. I couldn't bear the thought of sharing my personal space with anyone on a permanent basis. I'd had enough of that as a kid.

I think it's a sort of aesthetic thing with you, Sara said one day. I think she was right. I hated clutter. I hated mess. Other people meant clutter and mess. My apartment was sparsely furnished, all glass and leather and pale wood. Austere in its way. It gave me room to breathe.

It was the week before Christmas. For a while I'd been wishing I'd never told Sara about my imaginary place by the sea and my strange experience in the bell tent. That haunting sense of being stuck in a momentary timewarp between two warring factions. All that tension and fear. All that energy and exhilaration She kept bringing the subject up, wanting to know more about it, speculating about what it meant.

Why does it have to mean anything? I asked her. Why can't you just let it be?

It intrigues me, she said. I'd love to go there, see the place for myself.

There was no way I was going there. I'd last stayed there with Alan in the late eighties. The Janine problem was looming large. She was a nice kid but getting too clingy for words, the first female to try to take me over. I couldn't be doing with it. And now here was Sara, pestering. She kept asking me for more details of what we inaccurately called the dream because it was the simplest way to describe it all. A kind of shorthand.

I want to get the sense of being there, she said. It would be a great day to go. I reckon we'd be there in about two hours. Less than that, probably.

She'd long since convinced me that what I thought of as the watchtower was actually a folly. She wanted to see if there was a big house in the area, arming herself with maps and history books to find out everything she could. Her latest theory involved some sort of king called Maelgwn Gwynedd. She reckoned our camping ground had been on the site of a battle she'd found documented somewhere.

Give it a rest, Sara, I said. You ought to know me well enough by now to know you won't get your own way by going on and on.

Hey, she said, indignant now. I don't go on and on. This is the only thing I've ever asked you to do. And it's only because it's something that happened in your life that you said yourself was very important to you.

That's right, I said. WAS important. Ok? WAS not IS. Have you got that?

I've got it alright, she said. Don't you worry about that, and grabbing her handbag she flounced out.

After she'd gone I felt restless. We'd never had a real row before and it had got to me. Mind you all her obsessing about

the dream had got to me too. She was like a dog with a bone.
I thought I'd go out, just to get a change of scene, but then I
remembered she'd left her overnight bag in the bedroom. It
wouldn't have mattered but she'd brought clothes with her
that she was going to change into to go out tonight. On a girly
thing. It was Imogen's birthday and they were doing something special. Imogen was one of her housemates, the viola
player I think. Although I'd met them several times I'd never
worked out who was who. I tried to get Sara on her mobile. It
was switched off. I guessed that was for my benefit. I decided
I wasn't going to stay in just on the off chance that she'd come
back for the clothes. Why should I?

It was late when I got back. I was suddenly tired, had had
too much to drink I suppose, crashed out in the reclining
chair in the big picture window. That was the best thing about
living where I lived, the view. All the lights of the city sparkling
all around, the reflections on the canal, on that brilliant bridge,
the sheer style of it, on the Lowry Centre. The Imperial War
Museum. I felt satisfied with my life, with what I'd achieved,
with how far I'd come. This view, these lights, were all the
company I'd ever need. Just thinking that seemed to create
some kind of tipping point, or maybe the alcohol that had
briefly taken me up on a high now suddenly flung me down
again. I got to feel maudlin, even morbid. I thought of Mr
Pepper. The Indian tray. Inlaid with ivory. And Sara. Overlaid with irony. The words wobbled in my head like the lyrics
of a song. I thought how pathetic I'd been, never telling her
how Mr Pepper had left me his shop, and, more, something
I'd never known anything about, the terraced houses he
owned and let out. I wasn't the entirely self-made man I
claimed to be. I'd had a leg up to start with hadn't I? Modest
enough, maybe. But a start. And at the start, with Sara, I

thought she'd be impressed by my entrepreneurial skills. My investment portfolio. Property developer, music promoter. It had certainly impressed the others. But Sara was different. That was the whole point. If I got a bit uppity about my money and the stuff it could buy she soon put me right. Suddenly I missed her. I wanted her here. Sure, I hadn't wanted to go with her to the camping site. I don't believe in retracing my steps. I wanted to be with her, yes, but not there.

But what did it matter what I wanted? One minute I was watching my night world from my window. My penthouse panorama. My glittering urban stars. Then, without moving at all, I was transported elsewhere. I was pulling into the drive at the holiday camp, Sara beside me in the car. A bright winter day, the light sharp, intense, the outlines of things so clear. She was her usual enthusiastic self, had had her own way after all, though I felt no reluctance, didn't resist, just noticing how all the caravans were hidden from the road by trees now, how the gaudy inauthentic totem pole by the gate that I'd liked as a kid was no longer there, how the clubhouse had been extended, a swish conservatory all along one side, how the gravel was rich and thick under our feet as she led me by the hand as if she knew where she was going, through the calm empty landscaped park and through the little gate into the field. Here was the flat section where we'd pitched our tents. After supper on the last night we'd taken them down and put up the big bell tent. We could all fit inside this, and lying there in our sleeping bags, in a circle, our feet pointing towards the centre, we'd had a crazy raucous singsong. All the old-fashioned stuff. Ten Green Bottles. One Man Went To Mow. Does anyone ever sing those anymore? I'd fallen asleep in a state of perfect happiness. The week had been magical. I'd found my imaginary place made flesh. Alan was my friend.

All the others accepted me now. Better still, treated me as if I'd been friends with them for ever. And then I'd woken up with a jolt and found myself in a place that was the same and yet not the same at all. I felt for the first time the contradiction in what I'd felt back then. There was the thrill of the horses snorting and stirring, the jingling of harness. Weapons glinting. Banners whipping in the wind. All that. But at the same time there was a sense of detachment and calm. A pregnant calm at the eye of the storm.

I can see Sara now. Her sub-punk spiky hair dyed a weird but somehow attractive pinkish red. Her sub-Goth pallor. There's the tower, she said, her voice gone high pitched with excitement. She grabbed me by the hand with the eagerness of a child. Yeah, it's got to be a folly. Come on.

But we couldn't get to it. Efficient fencing and vicious barbed wire all along the edge of the wood. I'd never been up here. All those years back there'd never been any thought of wandering off on our own. Not allowed. Our time had been thoroughly taken up by organised games and activities. Besides, relishing all my newfound comradeship I wouldn't have wanted any solitary exploring. For me then the new yet familiar landscape was a brilliant inexplicable backdrop. I wouldn't have wanted to puncture it. It suddenly occurred to me – it might have disappeared.

You know when you were in the bell tent, said Sara. You didn't see your tower then, did you?

No. That was down there by the sea. We were camped up here. But where the stream is there was a kind of pool.

Sara laughed suddenly. The tower couldn't have been there then anyway, she said. It hadn't even been built, and wouldn't be built for centuries. Follies became the thing in the late eighteenth century...

And I realised how different we were, Sara and me. What had happened to me then, all the mystery of it, was just that. Mystery. It left me with a feeling of awe. And the energy I reckoned had been transferred to me somehow. That, pragmatic as I was, I'd used as fuel, to goad me on to make my packet. To buy my freedom. But Sara wanted to know. It was like an itch she just had to scratch. She always wanted to work things out. Explain things. Prove things. All that left me cold. But she wasn't finished yet.

You know how you described it, starting off with seeing the tents as pale cones. Remember?

Yes, I said, dragging out the single syllable.

And all that about the moon peeping out of the clouds?

Like a dinner plate. Wasn't that poetic of me?

Well, you were looking down, weren't you, as if you were outside the tent. And it wasn't a bell tent you were looking down on, was it? It was cones, that was the word you used. I see them as medieval.

Right, I said. I'd really had enough of this. You can't get all forensic with a dream. It's ridiculous. God, it was all so convoluted. And misplaced...

And then you're on the inside of the tent again. And you see the horses and the riders and the flags and everything on the walls of the tent. As if they're superimposed. Then you see the water, even the birds on the water, and now you're outside the tent again, aren't you? Or rather the two positions are fused. Multiple viewpoints. Fascinating.

And then I cut my chin on the tag of the zip, I say, trying to bring her down to earth. I'm going to go up there, she says, pointing to the old farm buildings on the right. To get the lie of the land from that angle.

I follow her reluctantly. The field is rough and tussocky.

Very uneven in parts. I'm out of condition while she's like a mountain goat. A quick, vivid little figure clambering up to the ridge. I remember that dog barking in the night all those years ago. It must have been tied up somewhere in this yard. The place is abandoned, derelict, the old farmhouse boarded up. There are a couple of pathetic cracked wooden seats made out of beer barrels and as Sara moves past them a rabbit emerges, scuttling off among the weeds growing in the cracks. It all happens very quickly. I'm a good way behind her as she goes to the edge and looks out, shouting something to me that I don't hear, the wind carrying her words. And then she falls, like it's in slow motion. Has she tripped? Has the edge broken off under her feet? I know it's a steep drop and I'm running across the yard towards her but I don't get there because I'm suddenly jolted out of myself. Or rather back into myself, back to my apartment, back to my vantage point in the window looking out on city lights. And my mobile's ringing somewhere. Fumbling I find it in my jacket pocket. It's Imogen. There's been an accident. Sara's undergoing extensive surgery.

It was touch and go at first. Sitting in the front passenger seat Sara'd taken the full impact of a collision with a carload of drugged-up joyriders. Weeks in intensive care were followed by more operations, then, once all the internal injuries were taken care of, a long stay on an orthopaedic ward. She'd fractured her pelvis and her left leg was smashed. As soon as I got the go-ahead I had her transferred to a private clinic for long-term rehabilitation, cutting-edge procedures, the very best state-of-the-art treatment. Physiotherapy. Hydrotherapy. I was so glad I was able to make this contribution. Meeting her parents I reassured them I'd pay for it all. I realise now, and it's embarrassing to think the implications of this just never crossed my mind, assumptions were being made all the time. By them. And by Sara herself. Wrong assumptions.

I cared about Sara. Of course I did. I like to think I'd have paid for her treatment even if there'd been no row and no dream. Needless to say I never told anyone about the dream, and at least this time it had been a conventional one, no matter how uncanny. I'd fallen into a drunken sleep and all that had happened in the previous few hours had coalesced into that strange hyper-real narrative. Bizarrely Sara had got her own way after all. We'd gone to the camp, if only in my imagination. She'd done all the exploration and assessment she'd wanted to do. And then she'd fallen. The coincidence, the dream fall and the real-life accident, was all a bit hard to take. Let's face it, we'd never had a row before, not a storm out and slam-the-door type row anyway. I'd been thinking such negative thoughts about her. I'd been irritated, angry. Did I think all that hostility on my part had somehow caused the accident? Not for a moment. Did that make me feel any less uncomfortable, any less guilty? Not a lot.

Months went by. I went to see Sara every day. The clinic was like a five-star hotel set in parkland. It was summer by now and Sara was so much better. I can't say she was back to normal because her injuries had been massive and their worst effects were not going to go away. There were other changes too. Gone was the feisty, strongly opinionated woman I'd always found so stimulating. I was beginning to feel ill at ease with the needy, pleading and rather petulant creature she'd become. Still, her therapeutic team had done all they could. It would soon be time for Sara to face the big wide world again.

We were sitting on the terrace at the back of the building, looking across the lawns to the small ornamental lake, admiring the huge chestnut trees. Near us, above the broad stone steps, stone urns overflowed with tiny frothy white flowers and dark green foliage. It was all very civilised. I began to think that perhaps I'd had enough of my city-slicker phase. Perhaps I should reinvent myself as a country gentleman. I wonder if some fleeting expression of softness and sentimentality crossed my face and Sara misinterpreted it. Out of the blue she grabbed my hand, staring up at me with a look that was downright gooey.

I can't wait for us to be together properly, she said.

What?

You and me. You know. In your place. On the Quays.

I don't know what you mean.

I find myself cringing now as I think back to that conversation. Our last. I didn't want things to end like that. I didn't see why we couldn't get back to the way we'd been before. I still don't. Even at this point no one could accuse Sara of being slow on the uptake. She was aware almost immediately that she'd got it wrong. I'd always said that I was a solo sort of guy, and as far as I was concerned nothing had changed that. For a moment the fierce Sara was back.

Is pity all you've ever felt for me? she stormed.

No. Not at all, I said. I care about you, Sara. I always have. You know I do. If there was any woman in the world I could share my life with the way you mean, it would be you. Honest.

Just go away, she said, holding back tears.

I'm not going to leave you like this...

Just go.

Reluctantly I stood up, started to move, and then she almost spat the words at me.

And by the way, every single penny you've spent on me being here, I'm going to pay it back. It'll take a while but you'll get it all back...

Look, I said. I don't want it. I wanted to help. I really did. Stupidly I added, anyway, you don't know how much it's cost.

So I'll find out. I don't want your patronage. I'll get a job. I can pull some strings. Now just go. Please.

I went, but I didn't leave it like that. I didn't just roll over and take it. The next day I went back to the clinic. They told me Sara didn't want to see me. That must have been awkward for them since the staff there obviously knew I'd been paying for her treatment. For a moment I thought I'd slip round the back, try to see her that way, via the terrace, but it would have been humiliating if she'd called security. The following day I tried again but this time they told me she'd left. I went to the house she shared with her friends. Imogen came to the door and made it quite clear I wasn't welcome. Whether Sara was actually there at all I don't know, Imogen wasn't giving anything away. I let a few days go by before writing to her at that address, and later, desperately, I wrote to her c/o the university department. Nothing. Nothing at all.

Did she pay the money back? She tried to. Several months later I received a cheque for a thousand pounds. During the next year I received three more cheques, the largest sum being for three thousand. Then she must have finally taken the hint. She'd realised at last that I'd meant what I said. I'd never had any intention of cashing any of them.

Foxy

Into the cornfields of the Philistines the burning foxes run. Red gold of the foxes. Red of the flames. Gold of the corn.

I've decided to be me. I know it's living dangerously but I've made up my mind, this is me as I really am. All the highs and lows. Intact.

And almost immediately the dreams start. Ordinary daytime things become extraordinary night-time marvels. Fine, so far. It's when the extravaganza of sleep slips over into hours of daylight that the trouble starts. This time though, when the storm comes, I intend to ride it.

I'm an artist. Well. I used to be an artist. But the marvels became terrors and my well-meaning husband Giles persuaded me to get expert help. Those were the words he used. Dr Drysdale's expert help was very expensive but his prescriptions worked well. I had no complaints. For peace of mind I was prepared to jettison every creative atom in me. I was thankful for the calm.

And then I met Foxy.

I'm jumping ahead of myself. I must tell you how I came to this outpost in the mountains, this cottage at the end of a narrow valley in north Wales. Our home is called Cae Llwynog. Foxfield in English, but it sounds so ordinary in English. And there's nothing ordinary about this place. Its signature is slate. Look one way and you see nothing but the old quarry workings, the great heaps of slate waste that are almost mountains in themselves. It has its own kind of beauty. Its light and shade, its cloudscapes. I never knew there were so many shades of grey.

I didn't want to come here at all. We had our rural retreat in the Rodings, so easy to get to from London, so charming too. We still own it, but for the most part Giles rents it out to friends. And friends of friends. But why Wales, I said, nearly seven years ago when he bombarded me with estate agents' brochures and I was merely bemused. I don't think I ever quite worked out why Wales, but that didn't bother me. Giles could afford it. No problem there. And I was so chemically insulated against any form of intrusive reality it could have been anywhere.

And now it's me that loves the place, that hasn't been back to London for years and has no intention of doing so. Giles comes here only occasionally, sometimes with a couple of friends maybe, to do some fishing or just unwind, walking in the hills. They attend to their own requirements, exchanging pleasantries with me, nothing more. Everyone back there in my former existence knows Giles and I live separate lives. Perhaps the writers of society diaries would describe us as 'estranged' though they'd be wrong, I think. There's still affection between us.

I haven't told Giles that I've stopped taking my tablets. Not that he'd hit the roof or anything. No, he'd be so very calm and reasonable. But Janey, he'd say, don't you think it would be a good idea to ok that with Dr Drysdale? No, Giles. You know and I know exactly what Dr Drysdale would say.

But at least this time I've had the admirable and perhaps unusual foresight to cut down slowly on my medication, bit by bit over a period of weeks. Doesn't that go to show that I really mean business? For the first time in years I'm free of my chemical straitjacket.

And I'm feeling fine.

I didn't want to come to Wales it's true but when I got here (just for long weekends originally till I decided to stay put), I decided to learn Welsh. I signed up for one of those intensive courses straightaway. I'm no linguist, believe me, and I got nowhere pretty fast but I did develop a lasting interest in things Welsh, the history, the culture, the legends. I started to read Welsh poetry in translation and, here's the coincidence that so affected me, I came upon that famous poem about the fox by the Parry-Williams or the Williams-Parry fellow, I'm not sure which one, the night before I met Foxy. Well, it was her cub I met initially. He stepped out of the bracken like a little ginger puppy. I nearly fell over him! And he held up his paw as if he wanted me to shake hands with him. You know sometimes things are just too cute to be true. Ghastly word cute, I know, but there you are.

The fox cub was there for just a moment and then he seemed to dematerialise back into the bracken. I scanned the bare grassy part of the hillside beyond and sure enough a little while later they emerged, a vixen and three cubs. She stopped and stared at me, at a safe distance, admittedly, but quite without concern.

And that was my first encounter with Foxy.

As I said, I'm an artist. And what I'd hoped would happen happened. Even before I'd stopped the tablets completely the dreams came back. And the ideas, weird ideas sometimes, but I welcomed them all. Not that my first drawings were in the least bit weird.

One of the things you can't help noticing when you come to Wales is the chapels because even the smallest village has at least two. I should imagine there must have been terrific competition between all the denominations, Baptists and Wesleyans and Calvinists and Congregationalists, all of them striving to build the grandest and the best. Not terribly

Christian that, perhaps, and now as the increasingly elderly worshippers decline and die the chapels do the same. More and more you see these often huge places standing empty.

The quintessentially Welsh scene for me is one of an ornately pillared and porticoed chapel set behind railings and wrought-iron gates, with, in the background, a hint of mist and fir trees. And then there are those heaps of broken slate glinting in the rain.

Anyway, I started to draw chapels.

I went looking for them. Since I lost my nerve with driving I've taken to the buses in a big way, bizarrely irregular and infrequent as they may be. My chapel studies started as strict architectural drawings. It was as if I had to re-educate my eye. And hand. There'd been a time when I could execute the finest precision drawings with ease. Not now. It was painstakingly hard work. Then, as I grew more confident, I started to sketch more loosely, more in my original style. It was as if I'd had to get back to the mechanics of drawing itself and be sure of that before I could allow myself a freer rein. When Giles came up one weekend after I'd managed to produce quite a portfolio, I showed him them and was pleased, for two reasons, first that he liked them and was glad that I'd revived my former skills, and secondly, and most importantly, that he still had no idea that I'd stopped my medication. There was no real reason why he should have guessed it, since I was perfectly relaxed and contented, but in a way it did indicate how little he understood me. He didn't seem to make the connection. It didn't occur to him that it was strange I should suddenly take up my art again, after years of not even thinking about it.

Cae Llwynog stands on its own at the end of the valley, facing the village in an oblique sort of way, looking out on the hugest, grandest chapel you ever saw. Engedi. It was the first chapel I drew, naturally, as it was right on my doorstep. It's been closed for some years now. The few remaining members of the congregation must have rattled about in its vastness and running costs must have been punitive. I'm not surprised it had to close its doors for the last time and perhaps there's a moral in the story after all. Of the three chapels in the village, this, the biggest and the most grandiose, was the first to close, whilst the smallest and most modest of the three, the plain, whitewashed Gosen, is now the only one in use. Engedi is still an extraordinary monument, its facade being so over the top ornamental it takes some getting used to. Frankly, it's ugly, but so confident in its ugliness as to be almost endearing. I tried to imagine how the original worshippers must have saved and saved to build it, how they must have pondered over the builders' style books of the day, before deciding on this dubious combination of classical pillars and gothic stained glass in windows incongruously like port-holes, except for one quasi rose window dominating all. The whole thing looks sad now. It's emblazoned with FOR SALE signs, and more recently, and more desperately, MAY LET signs as well.

There was never a dull moment at Cae Llwynog. I augmented my chapel sketches with landscapes, moody mono-chrome things that wouldn't please the tourist but reflected the mountains more truly than sky-blue prettiness and sun-shine. And I took an increasing interest in the wildlife of the area, sketching that too, especially the birds; kestrels and buzzards and the wonderful ravens, nesting high up in the quarry terraces. They're so talkative, constantly chattering amongst themselves. In spring and way into our brief summer, I would listen out for them calling to each other as they soared. And how utterly different were these calls from the harsh croaks we commonly associate with ravens. They were notes of joy, clear as bells.

And all the time I was getting to know Foxy. If a day came and went without my catching at least a glimpse of her I felt quite bereft. I would often go walking up in the hills behind Cae Llwynog, looking for her in a way I suppose, though at first it hadn't seemed that straightforward. I had only recently acquired the confidence to go walking on my own. To make me feel really safe I always took my grandfather's walking stick along with me, my talisman. It had been kept all these years as a thing of beauty rather than for its practical application, but practical it most certainly was nonetheless and I loved its smooth dark wood, its shape, its fine sense of balance and its band of enscrolled silver: I felt it brought me luck.

I'd been reading about Australian aboriginal art in one of the journals I'd started subscribing to again. The article was a bit of a hybrid, part artistic critique, part anthropology, but I was fascinated by what it said about the way those truly native people acquire their totems. They don't choose their totems. Their totems choose them. Surely Foxy had chosen me. I found this whole idea thrilling. I watched her and her little family with growing fascination. I found places where it was easy simply to sit and wait for her to come by. I never tried to hide from her at all. I got to know her body language, what I can only describe as her gestures, her means of communication and believe me, she did communicate. She was not in the least afraid of me and though I never tried to get too close to her and her cubs, I knew that on some level she accepted me. I was not an outsider, not to her. One evening I remember in particular, one of our special September sunsets turning the mountains into a paint box. I sat there quietly watching Foxy at the edge of the woods. We were both perfectly still, looking sort of sideways at each other. Then as the lightshow moved slowly across the sky the glory of it caught her magnificent white bib and turned it pink, no, more of a deep cochineal. She was thin, crumpled and shabby after all that breeding and nurturing, but still with her rich brick colour. Now she was regal. Just sumptuous. And still we watched each other. A mutual frank approval. I felt I accessed her pure intelligence.

I was conscious though, and not for the first time, that despite the proximity and acceptance of my totem, I could never be a true native. Love of a place is not enough. But even if my ancestry and my language debarred me from really belonging in human terms perhaps I could be redeemed by knowledge. I determined to get to know this land and the creatures of this land in the deepest way possible. It was not going to be just a matter of enjoyable country walks any more. It would involve a proper thorough-going study. I would keep a nature journal. I would observe more rigorously, not simply to enjoy the sights and sounds around me but to understand their interaction, their constant interplay. I would become a true ecologist.

The next time Giles came up he seemed to be rather amused by my acquisition of binoculars and reference books and my new interest in his ordnance survey maps. I thought he was being patronising and told him so, my earnestness alerting him for the first time that there was, maybe, a difference in me. He began to look at me rather quizzically, keeping his thoughts to himself, though, because Adrian Wallender was staying with us. Giles had shown him my portfolio of chapel studies and he was most enthusiastic. Adrian knows what he's talking about so when he suggested I choose the best of them and write a little history of the chapels, explaining the relevance of each name, for instance, and then send them off to *Resonant Image*, I was all ears. And then he said something about the name Engedi, and how it struck him as strange.

It sounds really Welsh, he said. Don't you think?

And it suddenly struck me too. Yes, it did sound Welsh. It was also unusual. The Horebs and the Salems and the Seions might be commonplace but Engedi was different, special, and, as far as I knew, a one-off. I had no idea what it referred to either, so next time I went to Caernarfon I found myself in the library poring over a Biblical concordance. Here it was, in the Book of Samuel, the story of David and King Saul, their enmity, and Saul's spies informing him that David was hiding in 'the strongholds of Engedi'. I liked the ring of that, and how while Saul slept in a mountain cave with all his men about him, David crept up from within the cave's depths and cut off a section of his garment, challenging him later by holding up the piece of cloth to prove how easily he might have killed the sleeping king. Why did this story appeal so much to our valley's quarrymen that they named their proud new chapel after it? I was none the wiser, unless they too thought the word had a Welsh sound to it, and liked, as I did, the idea of the 'strongholds'. For surely these mountains were still a language and a culture's strongholds, even today. I kept repeating the phrase to myself. It had an appropriately bleak, astringent music, did the strongholds of Engedi, with para-doxically at the same time, a kind of friendliness.

As I sat there in the library the concordance flicked open to a nearby page and I saw the word 'fox'. Quite casually I looked up the reference in The Book of Judges and read on, intrigued by an astonishing story of lust and violence and horrible revenge. I read with horror and incredulity about Samson gathering together three hundred foxes (now quite how did he do that?), setting fire to their brushes (the implication being that he did this rather as a chainsmoker lights one cigarette from another) and then letting them run loose, the poor panicking things, into the Philistine fields. It was the time of the harvest.

Red gold of the foxes. Red of the flames. Gold of the corn.

I felt that this was my image, that these were my colours. I can't explain it. I was exhilarated, appalled too, but I have to admit, mostly exhilarated. Something rushed up and out in me, like a log-jam breaking. I knew with growing excitement and conviction that this would become a painting, by far the best, by far the strongest thing I'd ever done. The background of it was there in my mind immediately, familiar as breathing.

Here was my stronghold of Engedi. Here was the view from Cae Llwynog, the row of quarrymen's cottages, with the circlet of hills behind, the stark geometrics of the quarry, the heaps of waste and then the chapel itself, handsome and new, a congregation descending its front steps following a sermon, a nineteenth-century congregation dressed in all their Sunday finery. A woman is prominent among them. She stands a little apart, pointing out across the valley, the foreground of the painting. It is one expanse of wheat. And it's starting to burn, but you guessed that. The painting has a split personality, half painted entirely realistically and with meticulously detailed control, half executed as a Dionysian welter, violently surreal. Half is grey, dark, wet, sombre. You can see the fronds of fern amongst the stones, the individual bricks in the wall. You can smell wet bombazine, wet gaberdine and serge, and the wet leather of hymnbooks. Half is an inferno, of stalks and seedheads, smelling horribly of burning leaf and grain, of singeing hair and fur. And amongst the corn run the glorious flaming foxes, consumed by their own fire, the colours of the sun.

I bought my acrylics, my boards. And I couldn't wait to get home. Did I know then that my latest craziness had begun? I think maybe I did, but if I did, I know, too, that I embraced it.

The House of Dogs

In winter the fields along the sea road are waterlogged. Fact of life. But when I was there with Alys it was already the end of March. Some fields were lakes with ducks sailing on them. Others were ribboned and latticed with water. Here, glittering, the water makes a shape like loose calligraphy. Long-billed and long-legged wading birds I can't name keep an eye on us as we approach the gate. Fly off slowly.

Then I was just a kid. Scared, not of my own shadow, exactly, though he would insist this was so, but certainly of my father's. He always seemed to be there, just behind me, ready to give me a clip on the ear if it suited him, though words were always his weapon of choice. What I see in front of me is now, but what I remember is then, and it's somehow clearer. In between the timber yard, that's gone, and the caravan camp that's grown, and is now so much more up-market, our place is still here, a long whitewashed cottage. The mismatch of sheds that had never heard of planning permission and the adjacent scrapyard, my father's kingdom, have all disappeared, replaced by a garden centre. Seems they make a speciality of fuchsias.

We stand at the gate and look at the wet world of the sea road, the stones of the embankment, the railway line. I have brought Alys here to show her where I come from. How can this be the place?

I met my second wife in St Ives, in the Barbara Hepworth Sculpture Garden. It was August, hazy and hot, people milling on the narrow paths so I couldn't take photographs. Parking myself on a bench I thought that if I waited till lunchtime the crowds would go. Strange what you remember, the small summer house with the day bed, white gauzy stuff with polka dots. It looked inviting. And then I must've nodded off right there, hey, anyone could've nicked my camera, to be woken with a start when someone trod on my foot.

That someone was Alys.

We made our startled apologies and that could so easily have been that. Later though, on the hot roof of the Tate, overlooking surfers on Porthmeor Beach, as I sat there enjoying chocolate fudge cake and coffee, she appeared. With apple juice. I called her over. We meet again, I said, surprising myself not only with the cliché but with my smile of real pleasure.

And that second fortuitous meeting was to bring me back here. Eventually. To a world of childhood memories, deliberately repressed. But repression is unconscious, isn't it? I'll rephrase that. Deliberately suppressed.

Back then, when I passed the dreaded eleven plus, things changed for the better. I became mobile and I made friends. Uncle Will gave me his old bike. Freedom!

My friends on Chalk Mountain were Hughie and Tudor. Hughie's father worked in the bank and Tudor's father had the Silver Fountain garage. We used to laugh that his dad was the car doctor, mine the car undertaker. I never let on how things were at home, though I think they maybe read between the lines. The scrapyard, anyway, was out of bounds for me. He didn't want me around and I wasn't complaining. I hated that graveyard of crushed and flattened cars, the smell of sump oil, of baked metal-hot to the touch. Condensed there too was that other unidentifiable smell that seemed to follow me for years, the total of everything I feared most and hated to the point of nausea.

Weird the way we're moulded, driven. I was to become a photojournalist, seeking out the world's wars and disasters. I saw things so terrible the car graveyard was positively benign. I made a name for myself. I made money. I married and had two children I hardly ever saw. Not surprisingly their mother divorced me. I lived on the deliberate edge of danger a strange charmed life. My father never knew any of this. He died when I was in my last year at school.

I was thirteen when we came upon The House of Dogs. That's what we called it, Tudor, Hughie and me. We couldn't call it the Dog House could we? Quite the wrong associations.

Summer holidays and we'd cycled for miles. The house was on the other side of Chalk Mountain, though by now we'd learned from Hughie, who was proper Welsh, that it's real name was Foel Wen. Here there was a huge quarry, and the trees in the little valley were grey with dust and looked half dead. The house stood on its own with only a rutted track leading up to it, the garden a scrapyard in miniature, rusted bits of machinery in long grass. On the doorstep there were rows of clouded milk bottles and a plastic crate. A stained, kapok-leaking mattress was set against the downstairs window in a vision of squalor, but the thing that got to us was the dogs. We'd heard their barking faintly in the distance but as we approached the noise exploded on us. There were dogs at the side of the house behind a worryingly flimsy wire fence, fierce-looking dogs on their hind legs, mouths agape with the sharpest teeth and slavering. And now, suddenly, there were dogs in the upstairs window, their heads leaning out at us, as if they'd like to jump down and tear us to pieces. We bubbled with fear and excitement as a man appeared at the door, shaking his fist at us and shouting, or rather squeaking. He had a peculiar, high-pitched voice. We didn't understand his words but got their gist. And scarpered.

Hey, I know him, said Tudor. Used to bring his van in till my dad told him it was a death trap on wheels. Even then he wouldn't give up on it.

Seems the man was known as Jimmy Baccy. Hughie had heard of him too, but had never seen him before. Knew that he had a cousin called King Arthur who wasn't all there. Mind you, nor was he.

King Arthur?

Yeah. His parents came from Cwm Sgwarnog way, Mr and Mrs King. Called him Arthur.

For a joke, like?

No. They didn't realise.

We thought this was hilarious. And we couldn't leave the place alone. All that summer it became our delight and our obsession. We spied on The House of Dogs, trying to get as near as we could before the dogs got wind of us. We reckoned there must be at least twelve of them, probably more. When the dogs started to holler we'd watch as Jimmy Baccy came out shaking his fist and squeaking, and on one occasion, jumping up and down in a rage like Rumpelstiltskin. He couldn't see us but he knew we were there. We were sneaky, creeping round the back through the straggly wood on the hillside, half dusty on the one side facing the quarry, green on the other. Then we wriggled on our bellies between the gorse bushes, finding a vantage point where we couldn't be seen. We were cruel and we were foolish. That last time, when he appeared with a shotgun and started blasting it off at the trees we nearly pissed ourselves.

You never mention your mother, Alys said as we walked back
to the car.

No.

Why not?

Good question. I gathered my thoughts. She did her best,
I said.

She had always tried to defend me, or rather devise ways to
ward off his words and blows, but she was cowed, shadowy,
becoming animated only in the safety of her brother's visits.
Will, in so many ways, was the one stable thing in our lives. I
used to have a few old photographs that showed a pretty dark
woman with long hair. I see her sitting with Will at the kitchen
table, chatting, companionable. My father left them alone, the
television turned up to full volume in the parlour reminding
them of his presence. He seemed strangely in awe of Will. In
the simplistic way of a child I thought this was due to the fact
that my uncle was a big chap, towering over him. As a classic
bully would, dad gave him space. But there was more to it
than that. Will was not just physically strong. He had an aura
of straightforward goodness against which my father's petty
cruelties withered into temporary nothingness. Needless to say
he was often particularly spiteful once Will had gone home.

For Alys I try to describe my mother. Where the picture of
her should be in my mind there's nothing that matches those
photographs. They could have been anybody. It's as if there's
no room for her, my father being so dominant. Only a sense
of gentleness. A shape that's too small. It's as if she's another
child like me, a child that incongruously loves to polish the
brasses, the twin copper kettles, all those little knick-knacks
on the mantlepiece. I can smell the Duraglit, the yellow cloths
impregnated with the stuff, the strength of it catching my
throat.

It was only when my father died that she came into her own, selling the place, buying a modern bungalow, spending her winters in Spain. By now I was in college and seldom came home.

There's just one more place I want to show you, I tell Alys as I turn the car towards Chalk Mountain, passing the Silver Fountain garage, which now has no connection with Tudor's family and has lost its petrol pumps. He went on to become an industrial chemist. Polymers or something. Hughie was a primary school headmaster in south Wales somewhere.

We'd long since lost touch.

I expected it to be derelict. I wanted it to look like some rundown rotting homestead in the Appalachians. One of those cliché hillbilly landscapes we're transported to in films. *Deliverance* country. But we like hillbillies don't we? We can patronise them. Not the mountain men though. Oh no. They're really wild. They scare us. But we use the two stereotype extremes for the same purpose, to flatter ourselves, to reassure ourselves of how far we think we've come. Those places of inbreeding, dirt and ignorance have nothing to do with us. Those places inhabited by people like my father, not that far removed from the Jimmy Baccys of this world. I feel a momentary sense of guilt, of disloyalty. As momentary as it is misplaced? Maybe.

The quarry had been closed for years, I knew that, and as we turned into the narrow valley I saw that the trees had lost their patina of dust and were in healthy bud. The house, recognisably the same structure, had been transformed. The garden really was a garden. It even had a children's swing in it. How could anyone live there? They've got to be incomers, I told myself. No one local would want to live there, surely?

Not after what had happened. And then I remembered it was more than thirty years ago. The house could have changed hands many times for all I knew, and memories fade. Not for us though. Hughie and Tudor and I had carried our guilty secret all this time. Or was I the only one of our trio who had kept it to myself?

It was a long splendid summer, the summer of The House of Dogs. Even after we'd started back in school the weather was still hot and bright, the skies cloudless. It changed dramatically for us one Monday morning in early October. Above the breakfast clatter I heard the news, the radio announcing that the bodies of two men had been found in an isolated house near Foel Wen. I just knew, immediately, instinctively, and I remember hearing, though with no sense of relief, that the police were not looking for anyone else in connection with the incident. No? What about us? Somebody surely would know about us? Bloody hell, my father said. Jimmy Baccy's gone off his head with that shotgun at last, has he? Always thought he would.

I had seldom seen him look more cheerful. Raging inside, I had the sudden image of myself standing in the doorway with a shotgun, my father dead at my feet.

Who would the other man be, then? my mother asked. The spice of disaster had made them unusually conversational.

That King Arthur, for sure, my father said. Since old Mrs King's gone he's been living up there. What a pair! Mind you, having him around would make anyone go round the twist.

I doubt if I'd ever hated him so much. He felt no concern at the enormity of this event. His callousness cut through me. Of course I knew he never had a good word for anybody, but even so his levity, his pleasure in other people's pain was never more clearly revealed. I knew exactly what had happened. It was as if I was there, seeing the chaos inside the house, the bodies lying where they'd fallen. The blood, the splattered brains. And I saw the dogs, some dead behind their wire fence, others injured, howling. I smelt it.

How? How did I know then that he'd turned on his dogs?

I was right, anyway. That's exactly what he'd done, but some had got away, lying low in the jungle of his garden, amongst the straggling bushes, the dank trees. The dogs were dangerous, it was decided, a police marksman being called in to finish them off.

At school we huddled together on the benches in the cloak-room.

D'you think it was our fault? Hughie asked. This was what we'd all been thinking, waiting for someone to mouth our fears.

No, said Tudor. I mean, if it'd happened just after we'd been there, maybe. But it's more than a month since.

That was the time he had the shotgun, said Hughie.

We were silent for a moment. Perhaps he was waiting for us, I said. Every day, maybe. Just waiting for us to come back.

But we didn't do anything, did we? said Tudor. Not really. I mean it was just the dogs barking and that, wasn't it?

None of us was convinced. School seemed a hostile place, full of this vicious and violent news. And all in our peaceful neck of the woods where nothing ever happened. The following week we read about it in the local paper. There was a pho-tograph of Jimmy Baccy and one of King Arthur too, though it must have been taken years earlier. He had the most pecu-liarly shaped oval head.

There's a real egghead for you, said Tudor. He might have just been trying to make us laugh, the way he always did, but it fell flat. Hughie and I just looked at him.

At night I lay awake envisaging the carnage I'd never seen other than in my mind. I was to spend my adult life in pursuit of similar images to that imagined one. I made a speciality of aftermath, only beginning to see just how pathological it was when some admiring critic dubbed me 'the aesthete of atrocity'. I started to think about it. Really think. Seeing, at last, how the tragedy at Foel Wen continued to have repercussions in the haunted life I'd lived. Any self-respecting psychiatrist would have a field day with me.

I was in the sixth form when I came home from school one day to learn that my father had collapsed in the scrapyard. I went with my mother that evening to see him in hospital and he died that night. I felt that I'd somehow been let off the hook.

I hadn't wanted to come back here at all. It was Alys who persuaded me. I want to know everything about you, she said. I was flattered, I suppose. And I realised that to her, the product of a conventional comfortable middle-class background, my origins seemed almost exotic. After I told her about the deaths we sat quietly in the car. What do you want me to say? she said at last, surprising me with the note of confrontation in her voice.

I don't know, I said. Nothing in particular.

No? Are you sure you don't want to me absolve you in some way?

No, I said. It's sorted. I got over it long ago.

She looked at me. I love that look. I can never lie to Alys.

I'm not a bit into psychobabble but even I have to recognise that there is such a thing as closure. And I learned from Alys, or rather she made me see for myself, how I'd hidden behind my camera for so long, using it not so much to see the world, as to detach myself from it, to be the permanent observer, neutral, uninvolved. I didn't go looking for disasters any more. That compulsion had actually started to fade out even before our meeting in St Ives. At the time I'd been in the middle of a commission to take a series of photographs highlighting al fresco art. The subtle pleasures of the sculpture garden meant texture and form, shadow and light.

More often than not now I leave my camera at home. I'd never managed that total neutrality I'd been looking for. Who can?

And now, who'd want to?

Advent

That mad woman, the one who's an artist would you credit it, she was there again today.

Oh God, someone tell her to shut up, said Sybil.

But there she was banging on the windows, yelling God knows what. And fair play, our Terry, like I know we always call him for everything, slimy bastard, you name it, he went out to talk to her, calm her down, not that he did mind, but that was the idea. He did try.

And how did I get involved? Because he thought I could talk to her woman to woman, that it'd be less threatening for her. What's more, he said, and it makes me laugh this, I am his senior operative. Senior operative, would you believe! Thought afterwards it wasn't so much his good will but that he didn't want to get the police involved, did he 'cos, let's face it, if they had a look inside they just might report him to the Health and Safety. I mean, things are a bit dodgy, and then he'd be for the high jump. And all of us with him, that's the trouble, and bang goes our Christmas money.

So here I am sat on the wall outside the chapel, talking to a mad woman. Or listening, really, as it's her that's got everything to say. Anyway, I was glad just to get out of that stuffy place for an unscheduled break (hey, that sounds good) and a fag, but I was interested in her too, got to admit. Mad people have got to be more interesting than us ordinary ones who go through all the hoops like bloody circus animals. Mind you, my Aunty Dilys, who was a nurse in Denbigh for years, said it wasn't so much that they were interesting or original or anything but that it was like a record had got stuck and you kept hearing the same old rubbish over and over.

Maybe, and she should know, though I bet all that old rubbish was interesting to begin with, before it got stuck in the groove. Dates me that, doesn't it just, records and grooves. Anyway, I'm sure this particular mad woman's harmless enough. And she's in one helluva state, all the sinews in her neck sticking out. Talk about agitated. Beautiful clothes she's wearing though. Casual expensive type, cashmere even, I wouldn't be surprised, though her hair looks wild enough to've been through a hedge and out. Her clothes aren't matching, either, and with someone like her it looks wrong. Forgotten all her colour co-ordination, she has. Like she's put them on at different times. And put other things on top. The layered look only it's not working. There's this long skirt, a soft brushed wool, pale denim blue, and a kind of pastel plaid blouse, lemons and greens. Then a long waistcoat-type cardigan, the shade they used to call mulberry. Still got an eye for quality, haven't I? Say what you like, I was a top machinist where it mattered, in Priestley's, before they pulled the plug on us and sent the work to Poland. Or China, was it? Whatever. Somewhere cheaper somewhere else. But for our Terry to call me his senior operative is just plain daft when all we're doing is sticking bits of card together. Still, we're all of us glad to have this chance to make some extra money in the run-up. Terry opens this place up when school starts in September and he tells us he's lucky to have such a loyal work force, tried and tested, all that, and how much he appreciates us. Takes us for mugs, in other words. He's always been good at the soft soap and the spiel, has Terry.

Anyway, I light myself another cigarette and let it flow over me. The smoke, and her too. The monologue. She's getting less agitated. I mean she must be worn out, going at it hell for leather. All het up about the name of the chapel for some reason. Engedi. Nice name, Engedi. I always thought that even when I was a little kid and they used to send me to Sunday School, me and the boys, get us out of the way so they could have a bit of peace, even a bit of slap and tickle, maybe, with us kids off the premises. Mind you, I only worked that out years later!

I know it's sad really for the place to be closed, but what did they build these huge chapels for? I mean even in the days when it was chapel three times on a Sunday and twice in the week too, they could never have filled a massive place like this. I reckon it was a kind of showing off. You've got to admit it's all upside down, say what you like, making Christmas decorations in an abandoned chapel. I reckon even Jesus has got to have a little smile when he thinks about it. They've closed his house where we're supposed to worship him but then they've gone right ahead to open it as a kind of factory just so we can make angels and shepherds and wise men to celebrate his birthday. Sybil says the mark-up on our efforts is something else, that our Terry's got some really classy outlets lined up for them, niche retail she calls them, and they are nice, you've got to admit, tasteful and that. The angels are taller and thinner this year and the wings more fiddly than ever to fix, but they look good. The wise men are in red and gold, rich and detailed looking and for the first time this year we've got friezes of Father Christmas and his reindeer, his sleigh full of brightly wrapped presents, all shapes and sizes. He's got an art student called Dorinda to design most of these and I suppose Terry's ripping her off like he does us. Still, he's got himself extra orders this year so we're working flat out and here we are in the last week of November. Last-minute stuff.

At last the monologue is easing off. She looks at me properly for the first time, making eye contact now, instead of preaching at me and staring sideways at me as if there's someone standing on my shoulder.

You do understand about the stronghold, don't you? she says, and why I had to do something.

Oh yes, I answer. Course I understand. I mean you're supposed to humour mad people aren't you? Go along with them, that sort of thing. She might be off her head but she's not stupid, not a bit.

You haven't been listening, she says.

I was listening, I tell her, feeling a bit of a heel now, truth be told. But your ideas are well, complicated and unusual... I reckon that might make her feel better. Not so much flattery, as a little appreciation. I wish my David had heard that. He always says I could be sent abroad to lie for my country. She still looks upset, so I smile at her, reassuringly. Perhaps you could explain again, I say, I didn't really understand about the stronghold exactly.

It's in the Bible, she says. It's about King Saul and David and their enmity. It's a quite wonderful story, actually. She writhes and wriggles her long hands. There's splashes of black paint on them.

Perhaps you'd like to come in and see what I've been painting, she says.

Well, I don't know. I mean, I'm supposed to be working. Then I think, oh hell, I'll go along. Why not? It's all in the line of duty.

Now her cottage is over the way from the chapel. The room she calls her studio is at the back with this panoramic view. But the painting propped up on the easel is of ravens, though mountains are hinted at in the misty background. Now I know about ravens because they make their nests up on the old quarry terraces and my lad Barry, who's very into what we used to call Red Indians (if I call them that he gets dead annoyed with me) says they're magical birds, very powerful. Well, they were powerful in this painting, believe me. You're very talented, I tell her. I mean it as well.

I'm just the channel, she says. The raven speaks through me, through the medium of paint, you might say. The painting is his really, you see, a kind of autobiography.

Right.

She seems to have forgotten all about the stronghold and I've got no intention of reminding her, but, just then, as if she's read my mind, she suddenly moves over to another larger easel up against the far wall. The painting on it's covered with an old sheet and she whisks it off, very dramatic and stands back. I don't know what to say.

I take a deep breath. That's the chapel, I say, my voice gone small and far off. This is the weirdest thing I've ever seen.

The strongholds of Engedi, she says. She smiles widely showing surprisingly tiny, little-girl teeth. Only the congregation, as you can see, are Victorian, dressed in their Sunday best.

But it's not the people standing on the chapel steps that have got my attention. Half of the painting is very detailed, realistic, I suppose. The other half's a complete mess. It's like she's tipped up a pot of yellow paint all over it, sloshed it up with red, like flames, and in the middle of it are these funny looking little stick-like dogs running around.

Do you know the story about how Samson set fire to foxes and set them loose in the Philistine corn?

Can't say I do, I say, and to change the subject, get away from the fact that there's something about all this that's getting to me now, I turn back to the normal half of the picture. That woman, I say, pointing to the picture, she reminds me of something.

This woman stands out among all the other chapel-goers. They're all in their best clothes, but she's different. You can tell she's very pleased with herself for a start. She's very straight and upstanding, kind of thing, with a tight, black bodice, a grey skirt with a full bustle and a pork-pie hat. Sounds ridiculous that but the effect's very smart.

I've seen her on a calendar, I tell her. That French artist who painted in little dots...

How extraordinary, she says. My mad woman's looking squinty at me now, but smiling more than ever and showing all those little teeth more than ever too. It's Seurat you're thinking of. He was a Pointillist. It's his most celebrated painting, actually: 'Sunday Afternoon on the Island of the Grand Jatte'. Then she says it again, only in French.

In that she's got a parasol 'cos it's sunny and you've painted her with an umbrella in the rain.

Well, yes, this is wet Wales after all. And I placed her there prominently as a type of homage. Ironic, of course.

I don't know anything about art, I say, and I'm smiling inside. I can see a change in her all of a sudden. People like to put people in boxes so they know what to make of them. So they know where they are. To her I'm just an ignorant woman who works in a fly-by-night factory. She wouldn't expect me to see what she's done, borrowing a person from a famous painting and putting it in her own. But let's face it, that picture was on the wall in my kitchen all through July. Or was it August? Our Carly always gets us a nice calendar every year and this year it was French artists. Impressionists and that. And the picture that made the most impression on me (ho, ho) was this one because it's all frozen and still.

You haven't put the pet monkey in.

Quite right, she says. But you'd hardly expect a pet monkey in a Welsh quarrying village, would you? Especially in chapel on a Sunday. Would you like a cup of coffee?

Thank you, yes, that would be very nice, I say. I don't say, well, you'd hardly expect a Welsh quarrying village on a Sunday to have a big splodge of yellow and red paint with little stick dogs running around in it, either. Even if they are supposed to be foxes out of the Bible.

We sit there for a while drinking our coffee. She's lost her uneasiness now. And there's no sign of that mad woman at all. I realise something. She's lonely. She's on her own all day long, no one to talk to. I wonder what she's doing here in the first place. I think maybe I'll pop in and see her sometime. If she wants me to.

When I get back to work Terry has a word, tells me I've got hidden talents, that the world of psychiatry doesn't know what it's missing. Maybe. Whatever. But the effects of my counselling genius didn't last long. She was an emergency admission to hospital that night. None of us at the factory knows exactly what happened, or what it was set her off again, but it seems that gone midnight she was out in the street shouting. She broke a couple of the chapel windows and splashed all the front steps with black paint. She'd run out of the red and the yellow I suppose. Next thing we heard was that her husband had come up from London and got her transferred to a private clinic down there. A couple of months later FOR SALE signs went up outside the cottage just round about the same time we heard on the grapevine that Terry's going to rent a unit on the industrial estate. That he's expanding. Going to launch a range of hand-crafted birthday cards and table decorations as well as his Christmas lines. And he intends to keep us on all year round. You've got to hand it to him, I suppose. Entrepreneurial skills and all that. I wonder what's going to happen to the chapel now?

Concerning Doves and Angels

I am driving from San'a to Ma'rib thinking of you. That day by the river, the day you brought me windfalls, yellow, bruised and small and tasting of cider. That bag you'd piled them in, frayed Indian cotton, pitted with tiny glittering mirrors. How you said they were diamonds. How you said there were alligators hiding in the deep parts under the willows. We lay under your alder tree. I can see its cones and catkins. Together. Why were there cones and catkins together? We always seemed to be laughing. You rubbed your hands with the flowerheads of pineapple mayweed, you knew the names of all the plants, and you rubbed my nose in it. Literally. I can smell it now almost. Musty and acrid, an elusive compound. All blended with sun and dust and dung. A dry path, leading down. Your river's darker mysteries made me try to compete. I said I'd learned to swim in our river at home. It was just a remnant in summer, but me and my mates had splashed about in it near the electricity substation where the water made a pool for itself before it slipped through the grille with a cool dark sloosh. And when we went to the swimming baths with the school we found we could swim. Sort of. We'd taught ourselves. How's that for enterprise?

I am driving from San'a to Ma'rib thinking of you. Another letter I will not write. There are lots of these. Can you feel them? The thoughts I beam to you from airports and hotel rooms. Those anonymous transit places. As if in those longeurs, the waiting times, I hold on to some vestige of myself by picturing you. But what picture is it? Not the bruised tired woman you've become. The girl you were. The boy I was. Are we the same people?

I've been driving for three hours. I love my wife, my son. I love my car. I smile. I love my job. Most of the time. Do I love you? What did I tell you? All those years later. That I was in petro-chemicals. You seemed impressed, so, with false modesty I said I was only some kind of glorified rep. Ah, but don't forget the glorified, you said. You were not taken in, saw straight off that I'd got a high opinion of myself. And why shouldn't I? I didn't have much of a start. And now with vast sums of money changing hands it's me in the middle of it and I can't believe it. You said you knew I was special. What did you mean?

This landscape is unreal. These mountains, these rock palaces, extraordinary decorative shapes, pinnacles with peering eyes; villages, little clumps of painted mudbrick houses on mounds standing in the middle of wildness. Fierce emptiness. And all the men I've seen, there aren't any women around, they're very friendly, waving, always smiling. But at the same time they're armed to the teeth with their bright and beautiful Yemeni daggers. Curves. Always curves. In the flourishes of their calligraphy. Scimitars. Crescents. I change the cassette, it won't do. There's no music to match this place, this mood. It's like driving into a film set. A timewarp. It's a land of brigands and secrets. Resonances I can't place. Promises I can't remember.

I switch myself away, away from this outlandish backdrop my car punctures calmly with its reliable hum. I'm moving through a membrane. I don't like it, so I think of where I'm going instead. To Ma'rib, to the newly opened oil refinery. That's better, reassuring since oil refineries are much of a muchness. International clichés. I banish the sense of being an alien in a foreign land by envisaging a complex of familiar shapes. Functional forms, cubes and cylinders, solids and sharp shadows, pipes and towers and hoppers, ladders and tanks, flurries of steam. Flares of surplus gas, asphalt and order. Why am I doing this? I'm always an alien in a foreign land. I like it. Usually. I mean that's why I've got this job. I'm good at it. In my element. But this place is different. It's getting to me. Eerie. A waiting, watching land. I'm half enchanted, half appalled.

Again I envisage the shapes I'll meet at Ma'rib. I give myself an aerial view this time. It becomes an abstract arrangement, a boy's wonderland and that old fascination works its magic. It always does. I think of my Meccano. When my father died his mates at work brought me dribs and drabs of Meccano, in shoe boxes, in brown paper bags. All these unsolicited gifts. I was snowed under. It felt as if all these assembly kits were meant to be some sort of compensation, as if I was supposed to reconstruct my father out of them. Come to think of it perhaps it was myself I constructed out of all those bits and pieces. I had to. What am I trying to say? The puzzle leaves a metallic taste in my mouth. I'm drifting again. A girl by a river. A boy. Music suggests itself, atonal, chiming, backed by the groaning and booming of nameless brass instruments, full bellied, ponderous. Now they bristle with valves and slides and I know I'm tired. I know my soul is tired.

Men and women are different. I laugh out loud at this profundity and my laughter bounces back at me with the scent of sunburned metal, hot leather, hot dust. But we were not different. You and me. It was almost as if we shared the same mind. For nearly seventeen years we lost touch with each other, but still we were able to pick up where we'd left off. Your marriage, early, disastrous. My marriage, prudent, much later, successful as marriages go, I suppose. If it's so successful though, how come there's room for you? But last time I saw you, you were cool with me, brittle, as if you could fracture in my hands, and I felt cruel, and guilty because I knew I was cruel. But still not guilty enough to stop the cruelty, knowing it was all I could offer you. You said you almost wished I didn't phone, didn't write. Well, I don't now, do I? Now Jill and Michael are with me in Abu Dhabi. A three-year contract. A residency permit. My prospects are excellent. God, how facile that sounds. Where does all this introspection come from? This isn't the way I operate at all.

And now it's Erin's turn to laugh. If you can call it laughter. From memories of his conversation, tantalising clues, tiny hints that might, just might have meant something, from the occasional gnomic remark on a postcard from some faraway place, (he was showing off wasn't he: successful jet-setting businessman sends postcard to naive little er, what would he call her? Mistress?) she'd built this baroque fantasy. It wasn't even her fantasy. It was at a further remove. She'd invented a fantasy for him, one she could share, slip into at will, as if she was thinking his thoughts about her, as if she was feeling his feelings for her. And all their ambiguities. How sad is that? But you know, the saddest thing of all perhaps, is that it didn't feel in the least bit sad. Self-indulgent, yes, delusional, very probably, but it's sustained her for years, this fantasy. Isn't that what religious belief does for people? An imaginal support system. At least she knows she's made it up. There are no illusions really. She's too honest for her own good.

And today that honesty broke through the whole elaborate construction once and for all. And in a paradoxical way it expressed itself in terms of deceit. It was premeditated too.

Bitter cold outside. And inside it wasn't much warmer. The central heating was on the blink, so here she sat, appropriately chilled, inner and outer climates harmonising. She felt that all this frozen winter beauty she'd been passively observing was somehow commenting on her own condition, fluffed up like a baby penguin, the collar of the big cosy mohair cardigan tickling her chin. It was a favourite thing to wear about the house but if she'd hoped it might serve as a comfort blanket it was offering none.

She heard a clicking tapping noise at the side of the house. With effort she rose from the table and moved to the side window, coming eye to sudden eye with a blackbird. So some other creature was actually alive in this frigid winter wilderness. The bird was quite unafraid and tapped again. Of course, the water in the birdbath was frozen like everything else and no doubt the feeders were all empty too. She went to the kitchen, collecting sunflower seeds and peanuts and a little cold left-over pasta.

Taking a deep breath she stepped outside. The cold hit her like a shovel in the face. The blackbird flew to the tangle of parchment-coloured clematis stems on the trellis, watching her intently with its shrill bright eye. Once the feeders were replenished she went back to the house for hot water in a big plastic jug. She also fetched a palette knife and a rolling pin, amused despite her forlorn mood at the incongruity of these objects. The water must have frozen solid almost as soon as she'd poured it in yesterday morning. Then she hadn't known she was about to hear from Duncan. She'd heard nothing for eighteen months not since he'd left the UK. The UK, why did that annoying expression sound so weirdly American? No. Yesterday morning she'd had no idea she would welcome his telephone call with what started off as genuine warmth, but

changed as she gathered her thoughts together, turning into
an almost entirely ironic performance. She hadn't known she
possessed such previously undetected reserves of duplicity.
Mind you things hadn't turned out as she'd planned. With
Duncan, did they ever?

The bowl was full of ice. She took the palette knife to it, not
expecting the ice to yield, imagining she'd have to smash up
the surface with the rolling pin and secretly looking forward
to this small expression of violence. But no, she just slipped
the blade down the side of the bowl and the whole thing
shifted. With a deft flip she turned it out like a pancake and
down it fell on the grass.

And it lay there, almost smiling, a glinting disc of ice.

This morning, first thing, she had watched him leave. He'd had
to scrape the ice off the windscreen and seeing him execute
this mundane, strangely levelling task, had made her soften
momentarily. How much more dramatic it would have been
if he could have swept off straightaway, undeterred by such
irksome irritations. When he finally got into the car he'd
amazed her, and probably himself, by waving sheepishly. Erin
did not wave back, embarrassed on his behalf. Besides her
arms were lead. There goes The Love of My Life, she
thought. Lately she'd recognised this tendency to retreat behind irony as a defence mechanism, but so what? Right now
she felt she needed all the defences she could get her hands
on. She didn't know how she felt. About Duncan. About
everything. And she didn't know how to cope.

These little frissons of sardonic anger that bubbled through
her now were surface phenomena only. Underneath she was
bereft, an old-fashioned word but a good one. Bereft. Altogether

it seemed bereavement was the theme, the *leitmotif du jour*. Tomorrow she would be leaving her comfortable semi-rural home in a village on the outskirts of Birmingham to face the wintry challenges of the real countryside. She would be going back to Alltgoch, the stone cottage in the hills where she'd been brought up. There would be several things to do before the house was ready for her mother's return from hospital. There'd be support from the district nurse and a Macmillan nurse. The doctors thought it would be a matter of months. Possibly weeks. They'd been very good at work, giving her immediate compassionate leave. For a speech therapist you're not always very good at communication, are you? Erin cautioned herself, as mingling surges of grief and panic swamped her. I hope I'm going to be up to this, she thought. There's so much to sort out in my head. So much to make a shape of.

Starting where? Perhaps with the templates. It wasn't as if she'd forgotten they were there, in the drawer of the bedside cabinet, wrapped around with stout rubber bands. The dove and the angel. Simple satisfying forms made of a light, pale wood. Balsa wood? She turned them over in her hands now, thought of how her father's hands had shaped them. Of the plan he'd had in mind. It was to be a labour of love, certainly. But such a fantastic creation, so utterly unlike him. He was practical, dependable. His movements were always careful and deliberate, their execution measured and slow.

Idris Jones was a joiner. He made his living by wood, and it was a straightforward living. Doors and window frames, rafters and fencing. Did he ever make coffins she wondered? She had no idea. Just a few days after he died she'd gone into his workshop, the sense of his absence almost physical, like the negative of a photograph. There was his workbench, scratched and stained. There were his tools, all clean and cared for. Her mother had decided Idris would have liked his tools to go to his nephew, Dyfan. Unable to face the task herself she asked Erin to sort them out for Dyfan to collect. Searching through some small drawers full of nails and screws she'd found the templates, had shown them to her mother who, for the first time since his death, had collapsed into tears. It was some years later before Erin had come to understand that these tears, and this response were not those of unalloyed grief, that it was rather more complicated. But there again Idris' magnificent creation, his *jeu d'esprit*, was itself a complex achievement.

The imaginative skill was undeniable but what exactly had inspired his vision of doves and angels? Erin thought of the Duncan fantasy she'd sustained for years. Did a relish for the fantastic run in the family? Especially where love was concerned? Especially when the personality in question was generally not given to flights of fancy? As a child it was all quite commonsensical and matter-of-fact on one level, but it had a magical component too. The background narrative to her childhood that always so enchanted her, even made her just a little bit jealous maybe, was that her mother, Theresa, was a gypsy princess. Why couldn't she be the gypsy princess? Anyway, gypsies have caravans don't they? That was the obvious bit, but this was no ordinary caravan. Admittedly only small, too small for any grown-up to get into, and bearing in mind that unlike any ordinary caravan, this one wasn't going anywhere, it was still the most beautiful thing in the world. It was completely covered with doves and angels, all created from these initial templates she held in her hands. The angels were painted with gold metallic paint, the doves with silver.

It was Erin's special present on her sixth birthday and

Idris had been working secretly on it for months. Delighted as she was with it, she felt, even then, that although it officially belonged to her, it had really been made for Theresa. That it was about her. That it told her story. But something Theresa had told her years later, on one of her occasional weekend visits to Alltgoch, a good while after her father's death, had put the cherished family mythology into bleak perspective.

As Erin grew up she came to realise that her mother wasn't a gypsy princess at all. It was just like when you stop believing in Father Christmas. But it didn't matter. There was still some romantic residue that Erin believed in. She knew Idris had been a confirmed bachelor and all of forty years old when he'd met Theresa, barely twenty. She'd known that their marriage had caused some consternation locally. But nothing prepared her for what Theresa had said one summer evening as she'd started to clear the table after supper.

I sometimes wonder if he ever loved me at all, she said. The real me. He had this silly idea of me, all that gypsy nonsense. And I played along with it I suppose. Perhaps I didn't dare rock the boat. I felt he'd made the story up because he didn't want to face up to what I really was.

Erin remembered the silence. She'd picked up the plates and moved towards the sink. There was a painful heaviness in her arms and hands.

I wasn't a gypsy at all. Nothing like. I'd been brought up on the road, mind. We were tinkers. Itinerants. Pikeys. Rough as hell, Erin. Travellers you'd call us now. Common as muck. That's what people said. And Idris picked me up in a pub.

Erin rushed to her mother as she sat at the table, put her arms around her and tried to hug her, conscious of a joint physical and emotional resistance in the rigidity of her shoulders. You were never rough, never common, Erin said.

You must never think that. And dad loved you so much. You meant the world to him.

But it seemed that Theresa was back there in the painful childhood of which Erin had known nothing.

They hated us, she said. Everywhere we went you could feel it in the way they looked at us. Sometimes kids threw stones at us. The police were always moving us on.

Erin didn't think she could bear it when her mother started to shake convulsively with silent jerking sobs. I couldn't read or write, she said. You never knew that, did you? It was Idris taught me. And I was never clean till I came to live here. I had nits in my hair. He must've been ashamed of me. That's why he made out I was this gypsy princess. That's why.

No, no, said Erin. You mustn't think like that. You were a real princess to him. He put you on a pedestal because he loved you.

She felt the stiffness ease just a little, then had the idea, half lifting her mother up from her chair with sudden urgency as if there wasn't a moment to spare. Out through the back door and into the yard, past the workshop that stood sideways on to the cottage, and on to the garden where the caravan still stood. In Idris' lifetime he'd twice repainted the doves and angels but since his death they hadn't been touched. The paint was flaking.

Just look at those shapes, she said. They're perfect, the whole thing's perfect. And who do you think inspired it? You. And when he thought of you he thought of the most pure and beautiful things he could think of, didn't he? Doves and angels. And remember his joke about the soft-spoken trees? He loved the trees, and he loved you because you were his soft-spoken Theresa.

Remember? Come on. Let's go a bit further.

Mother and daughter walked up the garden, up to the fence with the little kitch-katch gate in it, and on to the hill. That day it had been so hot, but now, with evening, a breeze had risen. As they walked up to the trees the memories were so strong for Erin that it was almost as if Idris was there with them. She'd been very tiny, holding his hand, listening for the first time to the clairvoyant speech of the beechwood. Trees are very wise, he'd told her. They know a lot more than us.

When they'd got back to the house, Theresa seemed settled and calm, Erin quietly congratulating herself on the success of their therapeutic conversation. Now, despite herself, she couldn't help thinking of the shock and chagrin she'd felt when, on her next visit to Alltgoch, there was no sign of the caravan. Prudently she didn't say a word to her mother. When Theresa wasn't looking she took the key to the workshop from its hook on the kitchen wall. She'd guessed right, and how forlorn it looked there in the cobwebby dark, the doves and angels almost sinister in the shadows. Had someone helped Theresa move it? It would have been heavy and awkward to negotiate it down the garden and into the yard. She had no intention of asking her about it so she'd never know. Neither of them mentioned the caravan again and in the workshop it stayed.

It was getting even colder. Erin put the templates back in the drawer. She switched her thoughts to practical matters, She'd have to get a heating engineer to see to the central heating before she left. Admittedly, if she set off tomorrow, which was what she'd intended, she might not be back till when, the summer? But it still needed to be seen to. Even as she thought about this she had to acknowledge that what she was doing was actually measuring the time until her mother's death. It sounded brutal but she knew, too, that with Theresa gone she'd have to sell the cottage. She didn't see herself as a second-home owner. Much as she loved the place she'd soon be saying goodbye.

Perhaps she'd be saying goodbye to a few more illusions too. Theresa's old notion that Idris had built up the gypsy princess story because he was ashamed of her. Could there have been some truth in that after all? Perhaps the demolition job she'd just done on Duncan, or rather, she reprimanded herself, her idea of Duncan, had given her a sudden taste for deconstruction. When Theresa had admitted that she'd never tackled Idris about the gypsy fantasy because she didn't want to 'rock the boat', could it be that the great love story she treasured was really a much more prosaic transaction? A shy, naive bachelor is swept off his feet by, what? A predatory minx with an eye for the main chance? And if all these things were true, did it matter? However, well, unusual the initial arrangement, Idris and Theresa had been happy together, hadn't they? But who can say? Who can ever truly know what other people think and feel, how much they care about each other, how much they love each other? All Erin could say, and all that had mattered to her as a child, all that ever mattered to any child, was that her mummy and daddy were kind people who loved her. And that she felt safe with them. And precious.

She thought of Duncan, whose experience had been so different. In those incomparably vivid first few months he'd told her a few things about his childhood with the nonchalant matter of factness she'd found so attractive. His mother had 'cleared off ' (his words) when he was small and he barely remembered her. His father had been electrocuted at work when Duncan was ten years old. He'd been brought up then by a stern, humourless aunt. Erin had met her just the once and had felt herself wilt under her scrutiny. In her mind's eye now she saw Duncan scraping the ice off the windscreen again. She saw his awkward, embarrassed wave. She knew on some level that what she'd seen wasn't Duncan the man at all but the relic of the unsure child resurfacing. And then she felt a bit guilty.

But in her defensively bleak and cynical mood Duncan's inner child joined up with the doves and angels and the whole notion of soft-spoken trees and placed itself in a mental storage box labelled *False and Contrived*. Or better, because more neutral, *Artificial*. She hoped the box was to be temporary even if it was, for the time being, necessary. Still, she wished she could walk in the beechwood now and listen to the wind in the leaves. Tomorrow she would be able to. She'd need the healing solace of the trees in the weeks and months to come. Didn't they say that the medieval cathedral builders had found inspiration for their soaring naves in the branching stateliness of beechwoods? She'd taken Duncan up there. They'd been no more than kids really. For a moment the defensive shield shifted again and some of that unmatched intensity wormed its way back. Wormed? Not a pleasant association. She'd really taken a pick axe to the whole thing, hadn't she? And yet she'd read somewhere, and had conceded its truth, that our earliest love experiences are hard-wired into the brain. Duncan had been well and truly hard-wired. No doubt about it.

She thought of the things she'd said to him this morning. Cruel things. He hadn't denied her accusations. He couldn't. But her own duplicity had left her feeling uncomfortable. When he phoned she'd said of course he could come. He sounded just a little bit tentative. After such a long time. Her imagination maybe. Duncan didn't do tentative. She'd welcomed him as if nothing had changed.

After a meal she'd prepared with her accustomed attention to detail they'd gone to bed. For the first time she'd made love with her body only. Not with her mind. Not with her soul. But with the icy, calculating intention of telling him in the morning just what she thought of him and that she didn't want to see him again. If she'd been the emotionally honest person she prided herself on being she would have said what she thought when he phoned. Instead she'd planned this pathetic revenge. Why? It hadn't helped. She didn't exactly feel like a million dollars. She couldn't even flatter herself that he cared that much one way or another. He'd have felt ill at ease because, just for once, he wasn't in control of things.

Never mind. It was done now and there were things to attend to. She spent ages just phoning around to find a heating engineer who could come today please. She packed then. There was a lot to pack too. Then she went next door to explain to the Claybornes that she would be away for an unspecified length of time. She told them the reason and they made appropriate sympathetic noises. They already had the key so that was ok. She also gave them all the wild bird food she had in stock, including some recently acquired niger seed she'd bought in the hope that it might attract finches. Not as yet. Her neighbours on the other side were new so she didn't bother about them.

The heating engineer would be coming after he'd finished all his other jobs for the day, so that left her time to do a spot of shopping for food to take to Alltgoch tomorrow. Rather to her surprise she found herself turning off for B&Q. Bleak and cynical you might be, she told herself, but you still retain some stirrings of human feeling She'd need to buy some gold and silver paint.

Strange Grey Weather

Strange grey weather is the name of the mood of this place. Other weathers drag their curtain of rain across the street or glint on wet acres of sand, the light so fierce it winces. Then there are gales of spite and thuggery, flinging rocks and green waves over the sea road. But what I remember is the stillness, that sense of being stifled by static air. The sense that something is going to happen, and it's not good.

I am standing on the South Cliff near the obelisk. Below me stretches the long shore, with the lifeboat station, the fishermen's cottages, the tall houses sea captains named for their ships; the Araminta, the Bella Ventura. Behind me there's a field where ponies stand at the gate. They are curious, squinting cross-eyed under forelock fringes.

You didn't tell me it was beautiful, Tim says.

I think I'd forgotten, I tell him, knowing it's not true. He knows too. He's so astute, Tim. Half the time I don't have to tell him things. He's closer to what makes me tick than I am myself.

You had to rewrite the plot, he says. So you rewrote the weather. And the whole appearance of the place.

Now I had to defend myself. Hey, hang about, I said. I described it accurately, didn't I? The basic building blocks sort of thing?

Yes, he says, as if he's reluctant to concede this. And then, after a long pause. No. Not really. How can it be an accurate description if you don't say it's beautiful? When it is.

I give him a playful punch as we scuffle down the summer

path. The scent of gorse, a hint of salt, a wind balmed with colours. And a pony whinnying behind us as if to say what about me?

I'd forgotten there could be weather like this. Classic blue skies, summer heat freshened by the breeze off the sea. Perfect weather. Ok. Perhaps I hadn't forgotten. Perhaps I was in denial all along. Lying to myself because it was necessary. Perhaps my idea of strange grey weather, that oppressive stillness accompanying it, was always more psychological than meteorological. If you set out to rewrite your past maybe you have to rewrite the weather.

You don't have to go through with this, Tim said as we drew up in the little car park by the lifeboat station.

I know.

Nobody's making you.

Right.

Tim walked on ahead on his own, on to the open headland, leaving me to my thoughts. He didn't want to influence me, make me feel that having come this far and having waited all these years it was written in stone now, a destiny thing. I'm still free to turn round and go back home.

But how could I do that now? A moment of return like this acquires a momentum of its own. A sense of inevitability.

Strange grey weather had become my defining memory. I'd preferred my own distorted version of things. I'd cooked the books if you like. I'd let a symbolic landscape govern my mind, my life, and its colour was grey. Even so there were many variations. It wasn't a seasonal thing. A grey day was just as likely to weigh down on you in the middle of July, though admittedly that particular greyness would be sticky and close. More often it would be November or February and all points in between, chilly and raw, damp creeping in to every crevice of the soul. There are as many versions of grey as there are of the truth. It all depends on the focus you want, the viewfinder you're looking through.

Just a few hundred yards from here there stands a detached between-the-wars family house. Roomy, four square, bow windows, pebble dash. It would be utterly conventional in a leafy suburban avenue but transplanted here to the seaside, with a row of tall, red-brick Edwardian boarding houses on the one side and a rather grand white Art Deco one-off on the other, it looks a bit out of place. This is where I was brought up. Here's where I lived the first eighteen years of my life.

Come to think of it, the village itself is a bit out of place in its entirety, a rag bag of buildings hailing from different times and constructed in contradictory styles, ranging from the Victorian homespun vernacular to what, in the 1930s, would have been the outlandishly stylish avant garde. And it's situated so bizarrely on what is effectively a bank of pebbles thrown up by the sea, a straggling street with long back gardens too salty and sandy for anything much to grow. They're more like tussocky thin fields than gardens really, all irregular in shape and strewn along the railway line. There's a quality of haphazardness and experimentation. Beyond all this there's a wide expanse of what was once marshland. Technically it's peat bog that's been drying up bit by bit for a hundred years or so, and as it's all below sea level it has an air of vulnerability. It's a marginal place. Looking at it now after years of denying its existence I can appreciate its uniqueness, its eccentricity.

When you delete a massive great chunk of your life there's got to be a reason. I certainly had mine, but over the last few years, since Tim came into my life I realise how drastic my response was. And has been. It shouldn't have been necessary. If I'd been able to talk myself through it maybe...

But there's no point thinking that now. In fifteen years or so the culture's changed so much. Nowadays if you stub your toe you can get counselling, can't you? Ok. I'm exaggerating but it's just amazing how different things are today. Mind you, the way we lived, the mindset was more Victorian than late twentieth century. Coming from my background, where nothing real was ever said, I can't imagine any way I could have behaved differently. Or been helped to understand what was happening. Eventually, when I punished my parents by pushing them out of my existence I was punishing myself too. And I didn't even know I was doing it. I can't believe how ignorant I was. I'd got myself pregnant at sixteen and I didn't know I was doing that either.

Meeting Tim coincided with my writing the words for a song. He was the catalyst, but he was utterly unaware of the effect he was having, of the way he'd broken through a log-jam that went back even further in time, to the summer following my GCSEs. I'd never written the words for a song before and I won't be making a habit of it. I'm not generally an expressive person and that's putting it mildly but somehow images and feelings long repressed burst through, turning themselves into marks on a page, the beginnings of a tune in my head. The context was one of safety and relaxation. This was the third of the Saturday sessions I'd spent with Cleo and Tim's team along with nine or ten kids from The Streets, an arts outreach scheme I was working on in Bristol. Only we weren't in Bristol. We were at Tim's recording studios near Malvern. We were making an album, collectively. The whole thing was funded by a Lottery grant. I don't know whose idea it had been in the first place but it was brilliant. Those kids, so many of them hostile and cynical at the start, or pretending to be, refusing to let down their guard, we saw them blossom. Visibly. Their faces changed. Their body language changed. I hope it did lasting good in their lives. It changed mine completely.

And I was only there by chance. Things can work out like that sometimes.

These were the words that started the ball rolling, that eventually brought me to this point, looking down at this place of my childhood, plucking up the courage to knock on a door, to see if I can rebuild the bridges I broke back then. To see whether, even when you think you've burned all your boats, you can, just maybe, start anew. Look at those metaphors. Burning boats, building bridges. Logistical military terms essentially, and so commonplace we don't even think of them as metaphors. Shows how often people have to do drastic things. To save their sanity. To stay alive.

> Ramshackle rainswept
> place between tides
> where time hangs pebbles
>
> I would go back to you
>
> I would welcome
> just those things
> I left behind.

Other bits of the song are coming back now. Damp salt amorphousness. Stonechats on fencing posts. There is something lavish, anarchic on the pooled shore, near the rotting groynes where they tethered the donkeys. That was a lie. There were never any donkeys on our beach.

Tim picked me up over one phrase. The bit that went:

by the railway line
barbed wire unravels

Have you ever seen barbed wire unravelling? he asked me.
I had to admit I hadn't. It was me that was unravelling.
Trauma is the repeated reliving of shock. It distorts you,
your memories, your whole self. It destroys who you are.
And it can bring about the kind of self-elected amnesia that
paints the remembered weather of your life in so many shades
of grey. Only now the grey was lifting. The colours were
leaking out.

I insisted on keeping that barbed wire in my song. It
belonged there.

We'd better get something to eat, Tim said, offering me
the luxury of banal comfort. Little spider rain. Just the tiniest
hint, so fine, so almost invisible it's almost not there. As I
walk with Tim in the here and now I feel the gentlest kiss of
moistness in the air, that smattering of rain they say sometimes comes with the turn of the tide, and there's not a cloud
in the sky. No precipitation in sight maybe, but there is an
almost imperceptible rumour of dust being dampened down.
The sea is far out, miles out it seems, so, somewhere at the
edge of it, where the sand stops and the waves begin, the
submerged clanking apparatus of the tides is chirring into its
old slow motion. Or maybe it's the far-away hydraulics of the
moon, that mysterious lunar mechanism exerting its sullen
power. I'm just being fanciful, finding things to think about so
I don't have to think about the important thing.

I was always good at that.

Gemma had been my best friend since our very first day in
primary school. The exams were over and we felt intoxicated
with a sense of relief and liberation. Her parents owned the

White Waves holiday camp. All through the summer she'd be working in the café there for two hours at lunchtime. When she suggested I ask my parents if I could work there with her I never expected them to say yes, but to my great astonishment they did. Straightaway my perversely cherished picture of them as fabled Strict Monster Disciplinarians begins to disintegrate but in all fairness to me, their reaction was most unusual. I think they realised, and appreciated, just how hard I'd worked and just how good I'd been, so they'd relaxed their usual strictures.

Apart from those two hours at lunchtime our days were our own. We could do what we liked. Needless to say we never told our respective parents where we were spending more and more of our time, convincing ourselves that as nobody had told us not to go to the Retreat we weren't disobeying them were we? Although Gemma was certainly more worldly-wise than I was, since no one could ever have been less, we were in our different ways both dutiful daughters. We really tried hard to be good.

The Retreat

It helps to frame it like that. To cut it off, exclude it from the ordinary.

Within the sense of the village mythology we'd grown up with, The Retreat played a special role. Our claim to fame. In the years leading up to the First World War it had been a mini artists' colony, ruled over by the patriarchal Samuel Woodfine. We'd seen photographs of him, grey beard bohemian, a Gandalf figure, with acolytes. We weren't St Ives, admittedly, but a few years ago a not-half-bad art film was made about this group of wealthy, footloose, free-loving and not untalented English men and women who descended on our unspoiled stretch of sand and sea to carry out an experiment that was as much social and sexual as artistic. A couple of miles beyond the last of the houses, at the far end of the long shore where the dunes meet the big skies and the wobbly Sarn road warns of subsidence, half hidden in a hollow in a tangle of willow carr, there stood a small settlement of wooden bungalows. Shades of the British Raj with their ornately carved verandas, maybe, or is it echoes of the deep South with swing seats on a back porch and mint juleps? These associations, mingled with images of the gypsy encampment paintings of Augustus John, have all been superimposed since on what were my own suppressed memories of that place and that summer, all fused with feelings of shame and anger and sheer incredulity. It seems so unlikely now. I can't get in touch with the person I was then. I don't think I was a person at all, just a bundle of naivety and confusion, not an agent in my own life but something that was acted upon by others. Utterly malleable. A silly little solitary babe in the wood.

Tim's voice and Tim's kindness cut in at this point. Stop beating yourself up, he'd say. You weren't that different from anybody else. Show me a teenager who isn't like that. Even the cool, supposedly streetwise types. Perhaps them particularly.

It was only by accident that we went in the direction of The Retreat that first time. Unlike Gemma I'd never owned a bike but I used to borrow one of those they rented out at the camp. We'd set off along the track that skirted the edge of the marsh and made our way to the church on its knoll with its windbent trees and its panoramic back view of the village. We liked it because it gave us a whole different perspective on things.

Only farmers' Land Rovers could use the track most of the time since it was usually muddy and potholed but in the middle of this dry summer the problem was the whirling dust, the coughing clouds of it that got in your eyes and chafed in your clothes. We'd sat in the shady cool of the trees by the church to eat our sandwiches and talked about the music we liked and the boys we liked though, even now I had some money of my own as I was earning a bit in the café, I knew I wouldn't be able to buy any albums or anything or choose the clothes I'd have liked to buy. Boys were entirely out of bounds for me, of course, but no one could stop me looking. Gemma understood and somehow got the conversation to feel relevant to me, making me feel involved and included, even if, in practical terms, I wasn't. Naturally she thought my family was deeply weird but most of the time she kept this to herself. She should have been a career diplomat, Gemma.

Secretly though, I hadn't got round to admitting this yet, I was dreading the sixth form without her. She wasn't staying on for A levels because she was going to the local college to study catering. I pushed all thoughts of school without her out of my mind, pretending September and the sixth form were still in the dim and distant future. I wanted to enjoy our special summer as much as I possibly could.

We'd freewheeled down from the church and were just making our way across the level crossing when we heard sudden high-pitched yelping. Immediately opposite there was a whitewashed higgledy-piggledy group of buildings in a sunbleached field where they kept hens in a neat little brown township of coops. A pair of frantic Jack Russells were tearing round behind the chicken wire as if this was the most world-shattering event ever to disturb the terrier cosmos. Their barks and squeals pulled us both into the drama as we saw a long brown lithe creature, fiercely alive, a stoat or a weasel though we couldn't get close enough to see, being tossed in the air, dropped, tossed and caught again, in a cruel circular game that had an infectiously feral relish in it. Twice the creature almost escaped the toothy muzzles and the swift short legs, as the terriers bumped into each other in their eagerness and stood there, silenced, momentarily disoriented. Their prey, obviously injured by now, tried to wriggle away in the grass. The whole thing was horribly ferocious and at the same time surreal, almost cartoonish. Time had slowed as we watched, transfixed, though it had scarcely lasted more than a few minutes, before, yanking away between them at the now increasingly limp brown pelt, the Jack Russells disappeared behind the hen coops and into the yard. How strangely white and empty the air was without them.

We'd had a taste of guilty voyeuristic pleasure, an inkling of whatever appetite it is that makes badger baiters or frequenters of dogfights pursue their illicit passion. We'd tapped into some dark undertow of violence, there to be found on the school field, perhaps, when the cry of *scrap, scrap* brought lads running down from all corners to witness the fight. Girls remained aloof to these activities, feeling superior to such primitive masculine demonstrations. Today we hadn't been looking for this kind of diversion, far from it, but brief as it had been, it had had its effect. A strange energy had bubbled up out of nowhere. The sound of it had hung on the air, the sight of it had focused our eyes on that bloody vividness. And then it was gone. Its absence lay around us like a challenge.

Neither of us had ever thought of going to spy on The Retreat. Over the years it had been tenanted briefly, now and then, the bungalows let out as holiday homes, but most of the time the buildings were boarded up, the grass around them grown knee high, the tangle of trees forever encroaching. We'd heard there were travellers there right now, that the police had been called in by some public-spirited busybody only to be informed by the great grandson of Samuel Woodfine himself that they had a right to be there. They'd been there all summer. We hadn't taken much notice. We weren't interested. But today, instead of getting back on to the main road out of the village, riding our bikes along the sea wall for an ice cream at The Lobster Pot or climbing up to the Obelisk for a spot of sunbathing, we found ourselves going in the opposite direction, further down the dusty track on the edge of the marsh. It wasn't a matter of making any kind of decision. We just gravitated towards the place.

A hundred yards or so further on there was a padlocked gate to stop bikers from town tearing up the track. There was a stile alongside and we managed to get our bikes over it. Not easy. Wherever we were going there must have been an element of determination in it, and I suppose it must have been Gemma who first turned her bike in the new direction. Wisely, her intention, if she even had one, had not been put into words. Being the goody goody I was, I'd have immediately said no if she'd suggested going to spy on The Retreat. But that's what we found ourselves doing. We thought they couldn't see us. Through the dappled light under the huge straggly split willows we were able to look down at them. The bungalows were built around a clearing where a group of latter-day hippies were lounging in old-fashioned deckchairs. There were three small children playing with a Labrador dog. It all looked very peaceful and harmless. Were these people crazy, druggy and dangerous to know, or maybe friendly, open and warm? The categories weren't mutually exclusive. We were to find out they were both.

Well, who have we got here? said this plummy voice behind us. The accent was very cultured and very English. There was nothing threatening about it. The tone was one of ironic amusement, appropriate enough as an introduction, that being the permanent mindset of Frayn Woodfine.

What sort of name is Frayn? I asked Gemma an hour or so later, as we made our way back home having been introduced to his merry band as mock captives, and made surprisingly welcome. The question had been rhetorical. I didn't expect an answer.

It's his mother's maiden name, she said. She's American. They do that. Use the mother's maiden name as a Christian name.

How d'you know?

I asked him, said Gemma.

We didn't go there every day. We thought that would be a bit much. And, prudently, we didn't stay there very long either, nervous of our clandestine excursions being discovered, but over the next three weeks or so our visits to The Retreat became the highlight of our existence. Lately I've wondered what it was we found there, and, more to the point, what it was we'd been looking for. Freshness. Difference. Rebellion. That for the most part by proxy, though Gemma did smoke a bit of their dope. Evie was the designated roller of spliffs. I can see her now, ethereal looking but with chewed dirty fingernails, her little boy Thomas standing beside her, glowering at us under his dark fringe. After her brief experiment with the weed Gemma announced calmly that she didn't like the way it made her feel. How I envied her matter-of-fact confidence. She didn't have to try to be anything for anybody.

Fair enough, said Frayn, smiling his ambiguous smile. But

the whole point about an acquired taste is you've got to give yourself a chance to acquire it, haven't you?

He was looking at me as he said this. Tell me something Ruth, he said. Do you ever do anything for the sheer hell of it?

I said something pathetic in response. I must have said something though I can't remember what it was. I was embarrassed, not just because I knew he thought I was timid and foolish, which I was, but because he knew I was fascinated by him. Infatuated from the word go, if I'm honest with myself, a new experience for me after years of denial and reinvention, and one that's not exactly comfortable. You start asking yourself questions and it's as if you've walked down a corridor with doors on each side. You open the door, get an answer of sorts, or a version of one, and then you're back in the corridor opening more doors. And then there's another corridor...

Recently I've found myself wondering if getting myself pregnant (I fell pregnant, didn't I? Wonderful expression that.) was a kind of revenge on myself for not getting the attention I wanted from Frayn. But that's ridiculous. The whole point about me then was I wasn't making decisions. I wasn't asking questions either. It feels now that I wasn't even conscious. Self-conscious, yes, painfully so. Conscious in any meaningful sense, no. I wasn't stupid but I might as well have been since I'd always been compliant to the point of idiocy. Sorry Tim. You're wrong. I wasn't a typical adolescent. I hadn't actually started the process of growing up. I hadn't even managed to peck myself out of the egg yet. Why? Already I'm remembering, viscerally, why I had to cut myself off from home and the influence of home. Do I really want to unburn my boats? What am I doing here? Frayn Woodfine the Magnificent wasn't the father of my baby. Nothing is as simple as that. Now I hear ironic laughter off stage. Possibly his.

All in all The Retreat had a decidedly theatrical quality. Frayn was like one of those dodgy dukes in Shakespeare, the ones who set up a situations, give it a stir, go away for a while to let things develop and then come back to see what's happened. And do a spot of judgement just for fun. A bit like God really, that last bit. And as a child, believe me, I'd had more than enough of God to last several lifetimes.

You ok? said Tim, looking at me with concern as we come out of the restaurant into the dazzle of noon sunshine. I'm blinking, disorientated, looking out over glittering wastes of sand at a burning horizon of blue sky and a thin, slightly darker line of cobalt sea. But I'm not seeing what's in front of me. What I'm seeing is the estuary. It's on our left and the tide's out, leaving only the thin brown river remnant among mudflats. We're on the embankment, me and a tall thin boy walking along it to the heronry. Short grass cropped by sheep and small yellow flowers. What I see is herons hung in the trees like so much dirty washing, then, when Dabs claps his hands, a sudden commotion as all those grey rags in the green branches rise up in raucous circling panic. Then Dabs is kissing me and leading me down to Pant yr Hespin like a lamb to the proverbial. That's what it says on the stone gatepost. Pant yr Hespin. I know a pant is a little valley or a hollow. I look up the word 'hespin' later. It means a yearling ewe. Roof fallen in. Ribcage rafters. But peachy cream rambling roses are growing on a broken trellis on a south-facing wall and their scent is strong.

You ok? Echoing Tim now, that's exactly what Gemma said to me all those years ago, as we cycled back after our last visit to The Retreat. After I'd gone off on my own with Dabs.

He didn't try anything on with you, did he? she asks me. God knows what I looked like. I must've been in a state of shock.

Ruth, she says. What's the matter? That Dabs didn't...

I'm alright, I say. And I'm not really lying when I reassure her that Dabs hadn't tried anything on with me. I mean, he hadn't just tried, had he? He'd succeeded.

For almost seven months I keep my secret. I become a leading exponent of the art of silent retching. I know I must keep my weight down so it doesn't show. Although I eat normally when I'm at home, normally enough, so as not to arouse suspicion. I don't eat at all in school, saving my dinner money for a rainy day that's very much on the horizon now, surely. I have no idea what I'm going to do. I just keep my head down and concentrate on school. I hardly have anything to do with Gemma. She comes round a few times but I always make excuses. She doesn't understand. But on one level she knows it's because of whatever happened that last day we went to The Retreat.

She'd stayed with Evie, Rainbow and the kids while I'd gone off with Dabs to see the heronry. He was new, Dabs. There was a fixed population at the Retreat. Frayn, the three children and their mothers, Eli and his sister, Gwynnie, who was in a bad way, smashed out of her head on whatever she was taking. Eli tried to look after her. Then there was the floating population. They'd arrive without warning, stay a few days then leave with no fuss, with barely a goodbye, in clapped-out minibuses, or in vans painted with fading psychedelic patterns. One of these was Dabs.

In my memory he looks a bit like you'd expect Huckleberry Finn to look. And yes, I did know the Facts of Life in a rudimentary fashion, though what diagrams in a book had to do with this I don't know. There was no connection. He was skinny and, in his opportunistic way, really quite kind. Was it rape? I don't know. I didn't want it but perhaps I didn't make that abundantly clear. And I didn't believe it would actually go in. There just couldn't be room inside me for something that big. It was a teacher in school, Miss Lettwidge who took me aside one morning.

Could I just have a quiet word, Ruth, she asked. Is there any possibility that... whereupon I burst into tears. She takes me home after school and has another quiet word, this time with my parents. After Miss Lettwidge has gone things happen very quickly. I don't have any say in any of it. I'm whisked away to a place in Yorkshire where there are four other girls in the same boat, so to speak, and two large, fair-haired women, twin sisters, who have exceptionally large bosoms but who don't wear bras. They look after us. The birth takes place in a hospital in Leeds and after two days I sign the adoption papers and now it's the turn of my baby boy to be whisked away. There's a whole lot of whisking going on here. Soon I'm back in school as if nothing's happened. Oh yes, by the way, I carried on with my studies while suffering from my 'nasty virus' and it's at some point while I'm in Yorkshire that I decide what I'm going to do. I'm going to concentrate on my French now, read French at university and get a job in France. I shall become French. Well, that may not be quite practical but I shall do the next best thing. My parents will have no cause for complaint. I shall cause them no trouble. It's only when they take me and my stuff to university and drop me off at the halls of residence that I'll tell them I won't ever be coming home and that I don't intend to ever see them again. And I don't. Though my mother writes to me every week in my first year. And every week the letter goes in the bin. Unread.

I go to France. I become almost French. I work, to begin with, as an *assistante* in a *lycée* in Toulouse, later at a business school in Strasbourg. Finally I get a job I love as the PA to the chairman of a consortium of small vine growers. And then it all goes wrong. It starts after an incident with a stalker. Nothing serious really, and I don't think for a minute he'd have done me any harm. It's soon over with. A caution from the police and that's that. But something's changed. For the first time in years I'm not in control. I start getting panic attacks. I can't face going to work, become scared of my own shadow. M Letheule tells me to take some time off. Go home for a while, he tells me gently, unaware that the only home I have is where I am. Here. Now. I resign. I feel I have to. I stay for a while with Gemma and Iwan at their restaurant-with-rooms on the Powys/Shropshire border. It's such a healing place. I help out as much as they'll let me, in the kitchen sometimes, or waiting on, or looking after the kids. I'm useful and grateful, in awe again at Gemma's generosity. She was always the same. Kind, Stable. Strong. She, and now Tim, too, are the most unfazed people I've ever come across. Through them I've learned what my feelings are, why they're what they are, and how to deal with them.

A year or so after my baby was born and taken away from me I told Gemma what had happened. Why didn't you tell me then? she asked. At the time. When I could've helped. I knew something was wrong, then. A little later, she adds, intrigued, How come you didn't show? You didn't look pregnant.

I'd hidden the truth effectively until that day in school when Miss Lettwidge noticed the way I was standing, Oddly, she felt. Just a sideways-on glimpse in the corridor. Afterwards she observed me surreptitiously for a week or so. Something about my back, my posture. There was no bump visible. It was just the way I stood.

It was Gemma's indignation on my behalf that made me realise what I hadn't even begun to realise, that made me understand, at last. How could they have made you part with your baby? she said and, later, Of course it was rape, you big silly. I knew it was all to do with that Dabs...

I'm not sure, I said. I mean, he didn't hurt me really...

I can see her now, throwing her hands up in disbelief.

You can add forgiveness to her repertoire of virtues. When I gave her the cold shoulder as I tried to deal with the nightmare of my secret pregnancy, she could so easily have reciprocated. She didn't. She persisted in being my friend. And Tim. When he was obviously starting to get interested in me I played my usual trick of trying to push him away. He stuck around. Something M Letheule said about a client comes to mind. He watches as a dog watches, he said, ascribing his comment to one Gaugin made about Cezanne. Well, Tim listens as a sound engineer listens. Which came first? Was it his quiet attentiveness that originally drew him to develop his chosen expertise? Or was it the other way round?

It was the place I missed, I said. We're standing on the sea wall. I'm looking forcibly in the direction of the South Cliff and the lifeboat station. Ramshackle rainswept place between tides, where time hangs pebbles, I sing softly.

I would go back to you, Tim responds. I would welcome just those things I left behind.

Yes, it was the things, I say. And the landscape as a whole. Stonechats and rotting groynes. Barbed wire. All that lavish anarchic stuff on the pooled shore.

Where they don't tether the donkeys because they don't exist.

Strange grey weather even.

But not the people, says Tim, holding my hand as we walk back to the car. They weren't in the song.

Whatever my Bird is

Sometimes I know there's a great black bird hanging over me. I've never really seen it properly. It's always just behind me. Glancing sideways I can catch the shadow of its wings. I hold my breath.

I've never told a soul about it, except Beynon. He asked me if I'd described it to Dr Brewster. Course not, I said. And then we were laughing. I may be crazy but I'm not stupid.

Now it's summer I go to Beynon's every day. He's been my best mate ever since we were little kids. But in less than two months he'll be off to college, like I should be. I won't wrap it up. I went off my head. And if it wasn't for the stuff I'm on I reckon still would be. The black bird is a relic of all that. A reminder.

I asked Beynon did he think the bird was a metaphor of some kind. Metaphor, he said. Don't ask me about metaphors. I'm just a scientist.

It's deliberate, this, of course. He can understand all about metaphors if he wants to. He's trying to take my mind off things. Get me to lighten up. But I'd really like to know what the bird means.

Not that it's there all the time. There are long gaps when I don't feel it's there at all. Sometimes I think to myself that it's gone for good, but just as if it could mind-read, that's when it tells me it's there again, behind me. It's less threatening now. I always thought it was out to get me, this bird, the symbolism, the black deathly feel of it. That's kind of softened and changed. I think maybe now the bird's more my protector than my enemy.

It was there, hovering at the back of me, when I was cycling to Cae Glas that day. That's where Beynon lives. He's so lucky, living in a place like that. His dad's a farmer who's diversified. They've got caravans. They always had a few but there's more now. In the orchard they've still got a little flock of Jacob's sheep, along with all the hens and the bee hives under the trees. Their honey's famous. But the best thing is the stables. They've got hacking and pony trekking and it's great for that because once you've got to Cae Glas Wood you don't have to cross the main road again. There's sandy paths through the wood itself and then you can get down to the shore and the dunes. You can see the ponies go in single file along the top of the embankment. I used to ride with Beynon on the beach along the tideline. We'd be out in all weathers, but I've lost my nerve with the horses. Riding, I mean. I'm not scared of them generally. And I help sometimes, mucking out and that. Some people have been funny with me since I've been ill but not Beynon's parents.

I haven't mentioned the livery stables. People have kept their horses up at Cae Glas for years, but while I was in hospital a new girl brought her horse, Juniper. This was Karina and it was soon obvious that Beynon and her were an item.

I can share. I'm not selfish. Beynon said Karina was an excellent horsewoman. She didn't look the type. Very small for a start. Petite, you might say, with dark hair and sharp features. A bit too pointy if you ask me. Still, I could see what he saw in her.

I didn't feel hostile towards Karina. I want to make that clear. But that day as I was cycling along the coast road I could feel the bird's wings brush my shoulder. It was quite definite, and as it's never happened before I knew some form of communication was taking place. I got off my bike and propped it up on the hedge. As I did this two things happened. I saw Beynon and Karina riding along the bridle path that leads back from the shore and I felt the shadow of my bird block off the sun. Whatever the metaphor was I didn't get it.

I reckoned they'd be back at the stables by the time I got there, and I didn't let on I'd arrived. Thought I'd give them a surprise, but it was me that got that. I could hear them talking as they were seeing to the horses. Karina's clear voice. I don't know why you let him come here all the time, she said. Faintly I heard Beynon saying what I always say, that we've been friends from our earliest days at school. But he's so slow, said Karina. You know, so duh. It's embarrassing. Again Beynon spoke up for me. The drugs he's on have slowed him down. They're cutting them back bit by bit. She wouldn't let it rest. Let's face it Bey, she said, he's never going to be normal, is he?

I didn't hear the rest of it. Quietly as I could I walked across the yard, retrieved my bike and went back the way I'd come. I was cycling fast but then I had to pull up. My head was a mess. I was choked. I love Cae Glas, more I think than even Beynon loves it. Perhaps if you live in a place like that you get to take it for granted. I could never take it for granted. I loved everything about it, the trees shaped by the sea wind, the vegetable garden behind its wall, the espaliered pears. When I was a little kid Beynon's mum picked me one of those pears. It was warm to the touch. It's a south-facing wall and gets all the sun. Above all perhaps I love the airiness and space.

And I realised that even more important to me than my friendship with Beynon was Cae Glas itself. I felt that if I could no longer come here I would die.

From where I sat, kind of poleaxed, thinking in a panic of

Karina in charge and me not able to come here any more, I could see her and Beynon come out of the stables, holding hands. I still had every confidence in Beynon. But I knew, too, that Karina was the type to be very persuasive, that she'd drive a wedge between Beynon and me, that she'd work on him so subtly he wouldn't even know what was happening.

So I had to do what I did. I called my bird and he came. Immediately. I'd like to say that this time I saw him properly, but no, not even now, not quite. With a very quick sideways glance I got a sense of the bulk of him, the coppery sheen on his black feathers. And, for just a second, I saw the talons of a great bird of prey.

At the inquest the driver of the lorry Karina crashed into said that as she ploughed towards him she held her hands up in front of her face. She'd seen my bird, I knew it.

I sympathised with Beynon. He said it was strange I hadn't turned up that day. They'd come back from their ride on the beach expecting me to be there like I usually was. I told him I'd had an upset stomach so I hadn't come. I lied quite easily which I don't do. I mean I'm not a lying person at all but this time I lied and it felt like the truth.

She died instantly. Beynon heard the crash, the impact, running up to the main road, seeing the tangled mess of her little red Peugeot. He'd never forget it. What had made her drive straight out like that? I found it difficult not to tell him.

He's at college now. He'll be ok. He's strong, Beynon. Meanwhile I'm up every day at Cae Glas. His parents say there's a job waiting for me when I'm thoroughly well.

I think about my bird a lot. He's been gone a long time and I miss him. I tell myself, though, that if I really need him, he'll be there for me.

The Edgeness of Water

In the olden days it was different, but that's the whole point. That's what the notion 'the olden days' conveys. But perhaps I don't mean the olden days at all, but the good ol' days. Are they the same thing? But isn't there more than a little irony implied in the expression, the suggestion that maybe the good ol' days weren't really so good after all?

Nobody's born cynical, I said to Paul in mid-reminiscence last night.

Are you sure about that? was his reply, stabbing and twirling his spaghetti for effect. As he dipped his head he revealed a distinctly uncool comb-over. It's a while now since he was here but I'm shocked at the change in him. My little brother has developed an incipient paunch and that thick head of hair's thinning fast. He's lost some of his transatlantic swagger too. I wonder if that went when Miranda went. Perhaps it wasn't his at all, but something he'd borrowed from her. And her illustrious family. And has had to give back. I knew about the divorce. What I didn't know till this morning is that Miranda's become a Buddhist nun. Of the Californian variety.

Rickety was the house in its hollow under the birches, off the track where rackety trams drew loads of limestone down to the quay. Rickety chimneys, rickety roof stapled down and anchored with breeze blocks. Flipflap washing in a jungle garden, a dog's cooped barking, black hens scratching about in the dust, one of them pink and plucked already, poor thing.

The quarry's closed now. How long ago was that? Twenty,

no, nearer thirty years ago. Can't remember. I can only pin-point when things happened, place them accurately in that magnificent unfolding tapestry of time when I can attach a time-mark I'm sure of. The year I got married. The years the kids were born. The year Paul went to America to take up his post-grad scholarship. Then the year he married Miranda and we went over for the wedding. He was a different person there, with them. He'd re-invented himself. He's a different person again now but I don't think it's from choice. He's taken early retirement, he says. Has no intention of going back. Wants to buy himself a little place on Anglesey and go bird watching and deep sea fishing. He hasn't said anything about big game shooting which is something I suppose, so he doesn't want to turn himself into Ernest Hemingway. Good. Not that you could go big game hunting on Anglesey. Wants to write another book, apparently, but something entirely different from anything he's written before. Sounds fine. So why am I worried? I mean, apart from the fact that I'm a natural worrier. Born that way.

The quarry's been closed long since and the tracks torn up. And now it's a walkway. Very nice. Tarmac underfoot and benches placed at strategic points for the purpose of admir-ing the view. Very nice view. But not as good as the view from higher up, where the flagpole used to stand, the worn, black-ened patch where the big boys lit their fires. You could see the river buckle its old slow bends, the spire of St Stephen's, the acres of caravans, the eyes of the shining greenhouses. And the rickety house where those hens gave us such a graphic, if unsolicited, lesson in the workings of the universal pecking order, well, that's gone too. Nothing more than a smudge on a concrete square now. Not that we knew then that the pecking order was universal. I might not have tried to rescue that plucked and picked-on hen if I'd known. Got myself caught on the barbed wire and shouted at by the scary man who lived there. Since then it's been downhill all the way, folks.

If you lived in the village you didn't have to pay to get into the waterfall garden. As kids we got in the back way anyway, down the damp path to the stepping stones, through the field where the donkeys had ruined hooves, swayed backs, past the white cottages, their lithe scraps of border. We would watch the dipper duck and dance on the stones, knew where he made his nest behind long moss at the top of the waterfall. Do chicks hear in the egg? I think they must, but even if they don't, by the time they've pecked their way out of their shells they'll find themselves regaled by the deafening rush and roar of water. Even in the most drought-ridden summer the waterfall never dries up. Nowhere near. And the dippers are back! Last year I went with a couple of friends for a meal in the waterfall garden. As we tucked into baked potatoes at a white plastic table in the shade of the massive ash, I told them about our long-lost dippers. I can see Chris now, open-mouthed, pointing with a fork in the direction of a dipper flight-past over the water. To prove it wasn't a hallucination it flew straight back up stream again, just for us. Perfect timing and right on cue.

Like the good ol' days after all.

Paul made a valid point last night when I told him this little story. Perhaps they've been there all the time, he said, but you just hadn't seen them.

Perhaps I just wasn't looking, I said.

Perhaps you just didn't have time to look, he said.

Fact is when you have something special in your life that's accessible all the time, it stops being special and you take it for granted. To correct that, I'm going to make a solemn promise to myself that I'll take my arthritic knees up to the top of the waterfall at least once a week from now on. I've got to say it's strange talking to Paul again, I mean really talking. When he's come over before, and he's done so every two or three years or so, something like that, he's always had Miranda with him. She was never anything other than perfectly pleasant but I felt as if I was on my best behaviour all the time. Shame I won't be seeing her any more. Now that she's become a Buddhist nun it sounds as if she was actually a lot more interesting than I gave her credit for.

Here is the edgeness of water. No such word as edgeness but there ought to be. Edge isn't good enough, precise enough. What I want isn't a word that describes the physical location of the actual edge. I'm not interested in that. What I'm looking for is a word that tries to get the feeling of the imminent plunge. That immediacy.

I don't think I've ever been back before. Not the real me. Though Miranda would say there's no real me to come back. No essential self. Lately I've got really interested in Buddhist ideas. The core of it's a way of seeing and being in the world. I'm not interested in two and a half thousand years of cultural accretions, the esoteric, ritualistic side of things. Like any other religion (though for me what differentiates Buddhism is that, for the most part, it isn't like any other religion) it's got its schisms and its sects. In the process of becoming organised religions lose their initial spirit. That's their tragedy and their danger. They become fixed as institutions, as embodiments of social and political power. The great thing about the Buddha was when they asked him if he was a god he said no. When they asked him if he was a guru he said no. So what are you? they asked him. I am awake, he said. I like that.

Especially since lately I've come to see that I've been asleep for a long time.

Ok. If there's no essential self who is this person who's come back? Who's sitting here today, as near as damn it, at the top of the waterfall? It's a very domesticated waterfall, it must be said. But its edgeness is the same (except for scale, and scale's irrelevant here) as the edgeness of, say, Niagara. What I'm interested in here is the quality of water on the edge.

Now if water were conscious, surely it would pause before the plunge, savour the easy leisure of the horizontal before exploding into the vertiginous perpendicular. Water would relish its own white-knuckle ride, its very own white-water rush.

Pretentious or what? Perhaps the most valuable thing for me in coming back home is that I get myself cut down to size. All that self-deprecatory British stuff seeps back in. Though Ems insists Brits aren't anything like as self-deprecatory as they used to be. Then she castigates me for describing myself as a Brit. You're Welsh aren't you? she says. Why don't I own up and confess I don't know what the hell I am?

When I sat here at the top of the waterfall in the early sixties I used to wonder just what it was like to be water teetering on the brink. I guess I was a pretty weird kid. Weird or not, when I'd had enough of things at home (which, let's face it, was pretty often) and when I didn't feel like going round to Clive's or Robert's, I'd come and sit on my own up here. I had enough sense not to clamber down to its stony lip and perch there when it was in full spate. I knew it was always dangerous, that even in summer's lull when the flow was modest and undramatic, my parents would have gone crazy to think I was sitting here, precariously balanced on an edge that was usually, well, a bit slippery to say the least. The danger thing was part of the attraction, I suppose, though I didn't see myself as being daring and brave. I wish! What I was looking for was a quality of something I can't describe. And I've never found it in any other context.

I've known for a while, from Miranda initially, and from my own reading later, quite a bit about different forms of meditation. Mindfulness of breathing, the cultivation of loving kindness known as the *metta bhavna*, walking meditation. Different forms of concentration using a mantra or a visualisation, of fire, maybe a candle flame, of focusing on various forms of mandala and, yes, of course, contemplating water. There's even something known as waterfall asceticism. And here I was, a kid, involved instinctively in a spiritual practice I didn't know existed. Not because I was precociously spiritual, unless you mean I had access to that natural Wordsworthian spirituality all children are receptive to if they're given half the chance. No, I was just lucky. I had a waterfall on my doorstep. And I found for myself, quite by accident, the special magic of staring at water as it flowed, hovered and plunged. But it didn't really hover, did it? There was no separate moment of edgeness, no mid-point state. I suppose I'm asking myself what was the nature of its attraction for me. What did I get out of it?

Just a couple of years ago I said something about this to Miranda. First time I'd ever mentioned it. I suppose I was kidding myself we still had some sort of relationship. If there'd been a mid-point state in our marriage when the process of dissolution was still hovering in the wings, so to speak, or more pertinently, perching on the edge, I hadn't recognised it. There'd certainly been no mention of divorce at that stage.

I'd convened a faculty meeting earlier and we'd had people round for a meal. She was loading the dishwasher, standing near the window. I suddenly saw just how thin she was again. Worrying, after all her years with anorexia. She was supposed to have recovered from it, put it behind her, like, I was soon to realise, she was putting me. She turned suddenly. I thought she was going to throw a plate at me.

Why are you always such a fucking academic? she said.

Which is a bit rich coming from her when she's a fucking academic herself. Or was. Well, half an hour ago, this particular academic thought he'd like nothing better than go and sit again at the top of the waterfall and contemplate that archetypal tipping point.

So that's what I did, shouting to Ems that I was going out and I wouldn't be long. But guess what? When I've climbed up, what do I find? That there are railings now, so I can't get down there, though paradoxically, a kid could, at a pinch. And there's a notice.

DANGER
CHILDREN MUST BE ACCOMPANIED
BY AN ADULT AT ALL TIMES

Well, way back then in the good ol' days, we weren't accompanied by an adult. Ever. We were all of us free to fall to our deaths at any time. Consequently none of us did. And then it occurs to me that even in these days of ubiquitous Health and Safety Directives, to say nothing of that constant fearful backdrop of the rampant compensation culture, and sure, I know it came over here from the good ol' Land of the Free and the Home of the Brave, well, d'you know something, don't you think there's a kind of innocence in that notice? The assumption that if a child is accompanied by an adult then that child is safe.

I wish Paul would stop calling me Ems. I was really taken aback when he said it the first time. And he's just come back from his walk and done it again. Nobody's called me Ems since I was ten. On that significant birthday, double figures and all that, I made a proclamation. Emma was my proper name and that's what I was to be called from now on. Or else. I don't remember anyone using my baby name afterwards, not even Paul. He was all of six and a half then.

Anyway, I asked him why he was doing it.

I didn't know I was, he said.

Acknowledgements

Some of these stories were previously published in *Planet*, *Blue Tattoo* and *Magpies: stories from Wales*, ed Robert Nisbet (Gomer, 2000).

The now amended first section of the much extended story *The Great Master of Ecstasy* was a prize winner in The Rhys Davies Competition of 1999, appearing in the anthology *Mr Roopratna's Chocolate* (Seren, 2000).

An earlier version of *Whatever my Bird is*, then differently titled, was originally commissioned by M&M Productions.

About the Author

Glenda Beagan lives in Rhuddlan, Denbighshire. She was educated at the University of Wales, Aberystwyth, and at the University of Lancaster. She has also published two previous collections of short stories: *Changes and Dreams* (Seren, 1996) and *The Medlar Tree* (Seren, 1992) and a poetry collection, *Vixen* (Honno, 1996).